The Sheikh's Second Chance

Kate Goldman

The Sheikh's Second Chance

Published by Kate Goldman

Copyright © 2019 by Kate Goldman

ISBN 978-1-07726-018-4

First printing, 2019

All rights reserved. No part of this book may be reproduced in any form or by any electronic or mechanical means including information storage and retrieval systems – except in the case of brief quotations in articles or reviews – without the permission in writing from its publisher, Kate Goldman.

www.KateGoldmanBooks.com

PRINTED IN THE UNITED STATES OF AMERICA

Dedication

I want to dedicate this book to my beloved husband, who makes every day in my life worthwhile. Thank you for believing in me when nobody else does, giving me encouragement when I need it the most, and loving me simply for being myself.

Table of Contents

CHAPTER 1 1

CHAPTER 2 10

CHAPTER 3 21

CHAPTER 4 29

CHAPTER 5 38

CHAPTER 6 47

CHAPTER 7 56

CHAPTER 8 62

CHAPTER 9 68

CHAPTER 10 77

CHAPTER 11 85

CHAPTER 12 94

CHAPTER 13 101

CHAPTER 14 111

CHAPTER 15 118

CHAPTER 16 127

WHAT TO READ NEXT? 138

ABOUT KATE GOLDMAN **141**

ONE LAST THING… **142**

Chapter 1

"Is Pablo in his office?" Janet heard. She looked up from her desk and found Mateo standing before her. Pablo was her boss, and Mateo was his right-hand man. Whenever Pablo had an important decision to make, he often talked with Mateo about it.

"Afternoon," Janet greeted him. Mateo stared at her with his eyebrows knitted together. He had such a cold gaze. He had a scar on his cheek that he had apparently gotten in a knife fight. "He's in his office," she added. Mateo said nothing. He just walked past her desk and headed to Pablo's office, which was a few feet from Janet's desk. Janet shook her head. She continued organizing files that needed Pablo's attention. She was almost off duty and wanted to make sure the documents were signed before she left.

Janet rose to her feet and marched to Pablo's office. Just as she was about to knock on the door, she dropped the files. "Damnit," Janet muttered under her breath. She crouched down to pick them up.

"This Sunday," she heard Pablo speaking.

"I can get it done," Mateo replied.

"Who else will be with him?"

"His wife and daughter."

The Sheikh's Second Chance

There was silence for a few seconds. "Go ahead with the plan," said Pablo. Janet finished gathering the files and then got up to her feet.

"Even with his child in the car?" Mateo asked.

"Doesn't matter. If we miss this chance, then we might never get another. Just take care of it."

"I'll handle it discreetly without leaving evidence behind."

Janet wondered what they were talking about. She knocked on the door. "It better be important," Pablo answered. Janet opened the door and walked in slowly.

"I have some documents for you to sign," she said to him.

"Leave them on my desk," he said. Janet walked over to his desk and put the documents down. She looked at Mateo and Pablo. Their faces suggested that they were talking about something very important.

"They're time-sensitive," Janet said to Pablo before she walked out of the room. She went back to her desk. She knew Pablo was up to something, but she wasn't sure what it was. She had worked for him for three years. Pablo owned Jinco Exports, a company that brought food from Mexico into Texas. Janet was aware that they transported more than food. Pablo was part of the Jimenez cartel, and he had many shady dealings. They used the export company to move drugs.

Mateo came out of Pablo's office. He walked past Janet without saying anything. Janet watched him push the glass door and walk out of the building. Janet shivered. His presence was always unsettling. Pablo was up to something, and Mateo was in on it.

"Janet," Pablo's voice disturbed Janet's thoughts. She turned her head and looked at him.

"Yes," Janet answered.

"I need you to buy a new truck."

Janet raised her eyebrows. "A new truck? Is it for a new route or to replace one of the other trucks?" she asked him.

"Buy the truck, Janet."

He was acting strange, Janet thought.

"I will place an order tomorrow morning."

Pablo shook his head.

"Buy it before you go home, today."

"Okay," Janet agreed. "Is there a specific model you had in mind?" she asked.

"Just a large Volvo truck. It doesn't have to be brand-new. Just buy a second-hand truck," he said.

"Um, okay."

The Sheikh's Second Chance

"Let me know when you've bought it. I need it before Sunday." Pablo went back to his office. Janet proceeded to look for trucks that were available for purchase immediately. She found a second-hand fm12 Volvo online. She called the company to purchase the truck. She went to Pablo and told him about the purchase. He seemed pleased and said that Mateo would pick it up.

***

That night, Janet couldn't sleep. She felt extremely uneasy. She kept thinking about Pablo. He was acting rather sketchy. He was eager to get the truck, and he said that he wanted it by Sunday. Why Sunday? Janet asked herself. Him wanting the truck by Sunday, and his conversation with Mateo made Janet feel sick. She replayed the conversation in her head. Janet sat up quickly.

She had got it. Pablo was going to use the truck to kill someone on Sunday.

Janet jumped out of bed and ran to the bathroom and started throwing up. She felt sick thinking about Pablo's plans. He wanted to kill a family and didn't even care that there was going to be a child in the car. Janet rose to her feet and washed her face. She rinsed the sick out of her mouth. She stared at her reflection in the mirror. Life in the cartel was not for her. She couldn't work for Pablo any longer. Killing an innocent child was the last straw.

The Sheikh's Second Chance

Janet had to leave the cartel. The problem was, the only way to leave was in a body bag. Tears streamed down her face. She had applied for a temp job at Jinco Exports. She was good at her job and got Pablo's attention quickly. When he promoted her, she was so happy thinking she was doing good for herself. That happiness quickly turned into a living nightmare. She found out Pablo was part of the cartel. Knowing that chained her to her job for life. There was no quitting once you knew about the cartel. The only way to leave the cartel was by death.

Janet jumped to her feet and ran to her mother's room. "Wake up!" she screamed.

"What is wrong with you?" her mother asked.

"We have to go."

"Janet, go where?"

"I don't know, let's leave. Now, Mom!"

Her mother sat up and switched on the light on the nightstand. "You better not be playing a joke on me," she said.

"Mom, I'm part of a drug cartel."

"What?" Her mother laughed a little. "How would you have joined a cartel?" Her mother pressed her back against the headboard and crossed her arms over her chest.

"My boss is part of the Jimenez cartel and—"

"Jimenez cartel?" Her mother jumped out of bed. "How?"

"I didn't know at first. I thought I was just working at an export company, but when I got promoted to be Pablo's secretary, it meant managing all his affairs. Including cartel-related affairs."

Her mother ran her hand through her hair. "Tell me this is a joke," she said. Janet shook her head. "Why didn't you tell me?" she spat out.

"I couldn't, I was scared. I didn't want to drag you into it," Janet replied. She told her mother how the cartel used the export company to smuggle drugs into Texas, about the meetings she set up for Pablo. She was never present at the drug meetings, Mateo did that but all the paperwork and phone calls, she did that.

Her mother was silent for a moment. "Why are you leaving now? What did you do?" She started to panic and pace up and down the bedroom.

"He's planning to kill some people. He didn't tell me, but I heard him talking to Mateo about it. Mom, I can't keep working for him and be engaged in killing even if I am not doing this with my hands. I have to run away because he won't let me quit."

Her mother was silent for a moment. She wiped a tear off her cheek. "Okay, let's go," she said. Janet nodded, ran out of the room and went back to her bedroom that she shared with her six-year-old sister.

"Kim, wake up!" she said as she shook her sister.

"What is it, Janet?" Kim complained. Janet quickly packed a few things for herself and her sister.

"Put your shoes on," Janet said. Kim reluctantly put her shoes on. Janet grabbed a coat out of the closet and put it on for Kim. She took her hand and they ran out of the room. Their mother had finished packing. The three of them dashed out of the front door and into the night. They headed to the nearest bus station.

***

Three months later…

"I'm here for an interview," Janet spoke into the intercom.

"What's your name?" someone asked through the intercom.

"Janet."

There was a buzzing sound, and then the gates opened. Janet walked through the gates and up the driveway. She walked up to the big house. A smartly dressed woman waited at the front door.

"Hello, my name is Janet." She extended her hand for a handshake.

"Hello." The woman shook Janet's hand. "My name is Mariam, and I am the sheikh's assistant. Come with me."

"The sheikh?" Janet asked. She knew that she was there for an interview as a maid for a rich man but a sheikh?

She followed Mariam into the house. It didn't matter too much who she was working for; she just needed money for her family to live decently. It had been three months of living in shelters and motels and working cash-in-hand jobs since she had escaped from Corpus Christi to Amarillo with her family. Her mother had gotten a part-time job at a diner in Amarillo, but it didn't pay much. Finally, Janet had gotten a job interview as a housekeeper in Dallas. Her mother was scared for Janet, going to Dallas alone. She didn't want her to run into anyone from the cartel, but Janet knew their usual routes and that they didn't have any business in Dallas.

Janet admired the house as she followed Mariam. It was large and beautiful. From the front door, they walked past the stairs and took a right turn into the living room. Janet glanced around. The room was massive with high ceilings, marble floors and furnished with a U-shaped grey sofa with a black base. A huge chandelier hung from the ceiling.

"The sheikh will be with you shortly," said Mariam.

The Sheikh's Second Chance

"Okay," Janet replied. Mariam walked out of the room. Janet checked her reflection in the television to make sure that she looked neat. She had dressed in a yellow blouse and a pair of navy-blue trousers. She wasn't keen on the color yellow, but her mother said it complemented her light tan, and it made her look warm and friendly. Janet had put her curly hair into a neat updo.

"Miss Gibson." She turned around and saw a tall and well-built man walking towards her. He had neatly cut and styled jet-black hair and a rough stubble.

"Hello." He must be a sheikh, she thought to herself.

"Have a seat."

Chapter 2

Janet sat on the sofa on the opposite side of the sheikh with her right ankle tucked behind the left one. She had her fingers laced together. The sheikh leaned back in the sofa and sat with his legs wide apart. He was wearing a pair of grey trousers and a white shirt that complemented his physique. Janet was fascinated by the entire situation. She had never met a sheikh before; she had only seen them on the news. However, the ones she had seen on the news were older. This sheikh that was sitting in front of her was young, possibly in his mid-thirties. He had great bone structure and a nice caramel skin tone.

"I am Sheikh El-Masry," he introduced himself to her. His voice was deep but soft.

"Hello, nice to meet you," she replied.

"Let's get right to it," he said. "Have you worked as a housekeeper before?"

"No, but I have worked at a hotel for several months. My duties involved cleaning, room service and working on reception. I believe that my skills are transferable to this position," Janet replied.

"If hired, you'll be trained on how to clean to my standards."

"That's fine. I'm willing to take any training required, and I can assure you that I'm a quick learner."

"How old are you?"

"Twenty-six years old."

"Do you have a criminal record?"

"No, I don't." But I worked for a criminal organization, Janet thought to herself.

"I will run a background check, anyway," said the sheikh. He was handsome.

"Okay, that is fair," she said.

"Have you ever been fired from a position or given a formal warning?"

"No, I haven't."

"If hired, you're required to sign a non-disclosure agreement," he said. Janet was suddenly wondering if he had something to hide. "It is because I am a sheikh and because of that, people try to sell stories to magazines and newspapers. I need complete privacy for the sake of my six-year-old daughter," he explained. Janet nodded.

"I would be willing to sign the non-disclosure agreement. When I worked in the hotel, I maintained customer confidentiality. Actually, I have a six-year-old sister. I am so protective of her, and because of that, I would never do anything that would bring harm to your daughter," Janet replied.

"Mariam will be in touch with you regarding the outcome of the interview." The sheikh rose to his feet. Janet stood up quickly and extended her hand for a handshake.

"Thank you so much for having me," she said. The sheikh looked at her hand and then at her face, and then back at her hand. He placed his hand into hers. His hand was soft and warm. "I look forward to hearing back from Mariam with good news. If you hire me, I will work very hard and will not let you down, and I promise you won't regret it," she added. Janet was desperate for the job. She felt disappointed by the fact that the interview was so short.

"Mariam will see you out," said the sheikh. With that, he walked away.

"Um bye," she called out after him. Janet regretted the words as soon as they came out of her mouth. She didn't know what else to say. The sheikh made her nervous.

Mariam walked into the room as soon as the sheikh left. "I will show you out," she said to Janet.

"Yes, thank you," Janet replied. She followed Mariam out of the living room and into the corridor. As Janet walked behind Mariam, she couldn't help but analyze her. She was tall and beautiful. Her skin was a nice honey color, and it had a nice glow. She wore a black pencil skirt, a white silk blouse and a pair of red heels. Her jet-black hair was tied into a high ponytail.

Maria opened the door for Janet. "We still have other candidates to interview. I will call you as soon as the sheikh has made his decision. It should be within a few days," she said. Janet smiled and nodded.

"Alright, I look forward to hearing back from you," Janet replied before she walked out of the front door. She walked down the long driveway until she reached the gates that opened in front of her.

Janet pulled out her new phone that she had purchased when she fled Corpus Christi from her pocket. She and her mother got rid of their cell phones just in case Pablo tried to contact her or track her down. She went to her recent calls list and called her mother.

"Hello," her mother answered.

"Hi, Ma," said Janet.

"How was the interview?"

Janet groaned. "I don't think it went well," she cried out.

"Oh, no, what happened?"

"The interview was short. I didn't get a chance to tell him how wonderful I am and how I am the best candidate for the position." Janet sighed as she turned a corner.

"Maybe it was short because you impressed him quickly or he's a busy man. What was he like?"

"He's a sheikh! I met a sheikh." Janet was excited about that.

"Really?" her mother gasped.

"I was shocked too. The sheikh was very handsome but cold. He didn't smile, even when I smiled at him. After the interview, I extended my hand for a handshake. He almost left it hanging."

"Oh, dear."

Janet sighed. "His secretary said I'll hear back within a few days. I'm not going to get my hopes up," she said.

"Don't worry, my dear, I'm sure you've done your best, and he'll realize it. You've got a great employment history; it'll be advantageous for you. You'll see."

"Thanks, Ma, you always know what to say to make me feel better."

"I just say the truth," her mother replied. "What time is your bus?"

Janet looked at her watch. "2:30, I'll call you later," she said.

"Alright, my dear, bye."

The Sheikh's Second Chance

"Bye, Mom." Janet hung up the phone and headed to the bus station.

When Janet arrived home, she was too tired to do much. The journey from Dallas was a long one. She went straight to bed and just tried to forget that the interview ever happened. She was sure that she wasn't going to get the job. A short interview often meant that the employer wasn't interested.

***

It was two days after the interview and Janet was pretty much convinced that she hadn't gotten the job. She lay on the sofa, browsing the internet, looking for jobs. She needed to get a well-paying job soon so that she could look after her family. They were currently living in a motel because they didn't have enough money for a deposit to rent a house.

Suddenly her screen flashed, there was an incoming call from an unknown number. Telemarketers, she thought to herself. She swiped the screen and put the phone to her ear.

"Hello," she answered the phone.

"Hello, may I speak to Janet Gibson?" It was a female speaking.

"Yes, this is her."

"Good morning, this is Mariam, Sheikh El-Masry's secretary."

"Hello." Janet sat up. Suddenly she felt nervous.

"I hope I caught you at a good time."

"Yes, you did."

"Great, the position that you interviewed for has been filled," she said. Janet's heart sank. She had expected not to get the job but hearing it hurt.

"I see; thank you for the opportunity," she said.

"However, there is another position that opened up, and the sheikh would like to hire you for it."

"Oh?" Optimism filled her voice.

"The sheikh needs someone to look after his six-year-old daughter. The role involves taking care of her meals, taking her to school and looking after all her other basic needs. The role does involve some housework also. It'll require you to live in the house. The pay is $2,500 a week. Would you like to take this job?" Mariam asked.

$2,500? Janet screamed internally. "Yes, I think I would like to take the job," she said. All she could think about was the money. She could look after her family so well with that amount.

"Great, you would be required to start immediately. Would that be okay?"

Just then, her mother and sister walked into the room. They had gone to the store to get some food.

The Sheikh's Second Chance

"Ah, yes. I can be there later today. I'll get the bus to Dallas," Janet replied.

"That sounds great. We'll see you later, then."

"Yes, thank you." Janet hung up the phone and looked at her mother, wide-eyed.

"What? Who was that?" her mother asked her. Janet ran to her mother and took her hands into hers.

"I got the job!" she cried out and started jumping.

"I told you!" Her mother smiled. She had been reassuring Janet about her interview. Janet had been so worried that she had not done well at the interview, and her mother kept telling her that there was nothing to worry about.

"I mean, it's not the actual job that I applied for, but the salary is even better."

"What's this job, then?"

"I'll be working as a nanny, looking after the sheikh's daughter," Janet explained. Her mother raised her eyebrows.

"That's not an easy thing to do. It takes a lot to look after a child, especially one of a rich man. The standards of care are very different," said her mother. Janet shrugged.

"I know, she'll probably be spoiled. I'll have to cater to her every need and keep her happy. The money is too good to give up the job."

The Sheikh's Second Chance

"Alright, do your best and call me if you need any advice. I have raised two children, very well too." Her mother gloated. Janet laughed a little.

"I need to pack because they need me to start immediately." Janet turned and went to the closet.

After packing was finished she hugged her mother and sister and then bid them farewell. She headed to the bus station and got the two o'clock bus to Dallas.

During the five-hour journey, Janet wondered what her life was going to be like. She felt guilty about having moved her family across the state because of the mess she had created. However, Janet couldn't run away from Corpus Christi, leaving her family behind. They wouldn't have been safe if Pablo knew that she had run away. Pablo, he was probably looking for her after she hadn't come to work for three months and had disconnected her cell phone. She hoped that she wasn't that valuable to him and that he would not look for her very hard.

Janet arrived at the sheikh's house just after 8 p.m. One of the maids greeted her at the door. "Is Mariam here?" Janet asked.

"Yes, she is expecting you. Can you wait here for a moment? I will go and call her. She's just in the sheikh's office," said the maid. Janet nodded and watched the maid go up the stairs. Janet slipped her hands into her pockets and just sighed. She had her mini suitcase on the floor next to her and a backpack on.

She heard the front door open behind her and turned around. She saw the sheikh walking in. "Good evening. Thank you so much for offering me this job. I won't let you down," she said to him.

"Okay," he replied plainly. He seemed uninterested. A little girl walked in behind him and just stood next to him. She wore a pink dress and had her hair tied up into a ponytail. Her almond complexion glowed like silk. She looked at Janet and then at the sheikh.

"This must be your daughter." Janet smiled. The little girl pulled out a notepad from her pocket and started writing on it. She held it up and showed the sheikh. He looked at the pad.

"Your new nanny," he answered. The girl looked at Janet.

"Hi, I'm Janet." Janet held out her palm for a handshake. The little girl stared at Janet blankly and then just nodded. She walked past Janet and headed upstairs. Janet looked at the sheikh for answers.

"Rest up," he said to her and then walked off. Janet was left standing alone at the entrance, wondering if she had done something wrong. Both father and daughter seemed cold. She had noticed that his daughter didn't speak; she had written on a notepad.

Janet wondered why she did that. The job was going to be harder than she thought.

Chapter 3

It was just around 10 a.m. on Saturday. Basil and his daughter were sitting out on the patio about to have breakfast when Mariam and the new nanny walked outside. He wondered how long she was going to last. The last one had lasted two weeks before his daughter Sanaa decided that she didn't like her.

"Morning, sheikh," Mariam greeted him. "Morning, Sanaa."

"Morning," he replied.

"Janet is starting work today. I'm just showing her the house and explaining a few rules to her."

Janet. So that was her name, Basil thought to himself. It was a good thing Mariam had said it because Basil couldn't remember what her name was. He leaned into his chair and studied Janet. She was of average height, around five feet five inches. She was smartly dressed in a long-sleeved white shirt and a high-waisted black skirt and a pair of flat black shoes. Her hair was parted at the side and tied into a low bun.

"Good morning, sheikh," she greeted him with a smile on her face. She had silky skin with a light tan. Her figure resembled an hourglass.

"Morning," he replied. Janet turned to face his daughter.

"Hi, Sanaa." She had a big smile on her face, but Sanaa didn't return her smile. She had her notepad on the table next to her. She picked up her pen and wrote *hi* on it. She showed it to Janet.

"Hi, sweetheart, how are you?" Janet was looking at Sanaa, waiting for her to respond.

Janet seemed so cheerful. Sanaa quickly scribbled something down, hiding it from Janet and Mariam. She showed it to the sheikh. *She's weird,* it read. Basil almost laughed. Sanaa flipped the notepad after letting her father read it so that Janet wouldn't see.

"Make sure you listen to everything Mariam tells you. Looking after my child is an important job, and I expect you to do it well," he said to Janet. She nodded.

"Yes, sheikh, I will work very hard."

Basil just nodded.

"Let's go," Mariam said to Janet.

"I'll see you later." Janet waved at Sanaa before she and Mariam went back into the house. Sanaa shook her head before she started eating. Basil was not shocked that his daughter hadn't taken a liking to Janet immediately. She was just as picky as he was, and because of that, all the nannies he had hired since her mother passed away never lasted. He wondered how long Janet was going to last.

Basil and his daughter had breakfast after Janet and Mariam left. When they finished eating, Basil went into his home office to get some work done. His family owned an oil company in El-Tabas, a small country in the Middle East. Though they had other branches in the world, Basil was currently focusing on managing the Dallas one because he wanted to expand their business in the U.S.

***

"I am off now," Mariam said to Janet.

"Alright," Janet replied. Janet watched Mariam walk out of the front door.

Janet had spent most of the morning with Mariam getting an introduction to her new role and place of living. Mariam had shown Janet around the sheikh's house. The house was so big, it could pass for a small hotel. Janet had also received a list of foods Sanaa liked and disliked, and what she was allergic to. All that was fine for Janet; she had a good memory and could master things quickly.

Now that Mariam was gone, it was time for Janet to start her job officially. It was almost one o'clock, which meant it was lunchtime for Sanaa. It was Janet's duty to make sure that Sanaa had her lunch. Janet started walking down the corridor and took a right turn into the large dining room. One of the maids was in there setting up the table.

"Hi, I'm Janet," she introduced herself.

"Hello, my name is Ruth," the maid greeted her. She was wearing a calf-length short-sleeved black dress with a white collar. Her hair was tied into a low bun.

"Nice to meet you." Janet smiled at her. "I just came to check on the lunch for Sanaa before I go to get her. Is the food ready?"

"Yes." Ruth had a Middle Eastern accent.

"Alright, I'll go find her." Janet smiled before she left the room.

She headed up the staircase and then turned left. Janet headed down the long corridor. She stopped at the end of the corridor. There were two doors there, and Janet couldn't remember which one led to Sanaa's room. One of them led to the sheikh's room, so she didn't want to knock on the wrong one. She stood there for a moment trying to figure out which one it was. She spun around in a circle.

"What are you doing?" she heard a voice sounding from behind her. She let out a squirm and placed her hand on her chest. She turned and found the sheikh standing there looking at her.

"I forgot which one was Sanaa's room." She smiled awkwardly. The sheikh nodded at the door on the right. "Ahh, thank you. I was coming to call her down for lunch," she said.

"I see." The sheikh walked past Janet and opened the door on the left. He walked in and shut the door. Janet knocked on Sanaa's door before she walked in. The sheikh's daughter was sitting at her white desk with pencils and a coloring book.

"Hi, Sanaa," Janet greeted her. Sanaa rose to her feet and picked up her notepad and pen. She scribbled on it and then showed it to Janet. *Lunch,* it read. "Yes, it's lunchtime," Janet replied. Sanaa started walking towards the door. Janet followed her out, and they headed downstairs.

Sanaa walked into the dining room and pulled out a chair from the table. She sat down in the chair and then picked up a napkin. Ruth had just finished serving the food. She left the room immediately.

"Can I help you?" Janet asked. Sanaa shook her head. She tucked the napkin into her T-shirt at the collar. Janet went to stand by the window. As per Mariam's instructions, she had to be in the room whenever Sanaa was eating and had to pay attention to her. Sanaa picked up a silver fork with her left hand and started eating.

"Oh, you're left-handed!" Janet exclaimed. Sanaa looked at her for a moment and then kept eating. Janet cleared her throat. She thought Sanaa would be as talkative as her sister. However, that wasn't the case.

Janet watched Sanaa eat. The little girl ate slowly and wiped her mouth almost after every bite. She was only six years old, but ate neatly, unlike Janet's sister who chewed loudly and got food all over her mouth. Janet's little sister Kim was more talkative, clumsy and messy.

After she finished eating, Sanaa wiped her mouth with the napkin and then drank her water. She got up from the table and walked out. Janet followed her. They went to the living room and sat down on the sofas. Sanaa turned on the TV. Not long after they started watching cartoons, Sanaa started dozing off.

"Are you sleepy?" Janet asked her. "Shall I take you upstairs to bed?"

Sanaa shook her head and rubbed her eyes. She sat up straight and focused on the TV. She barely laughed or smiled. She started dozing off again. Her head rocked back and forth. She was trying to fight off the sleep, but she seemed very tired. Janet held Sanaa and gently laid her down. The little girl was obviously tired and needed rest.

Janet turned off the TV and then left the room. She rushed into one of the guest rooms and retrieved a thin blanket. She went back to the living room and covered Sanaa with it. Sanaa slept on the sofa so soundly. Janet sighed to herself. She felt so bad for Sanaa because of what Mariam had told her. A few months ago, Sanaa and her mother had been involved in a car accident. Sanaa escaped without any serious injuries, but her mother hadn't been so lucky. She had sustained fatal injuries. Since then, Sanaa had stopped speaking. She communicated through her notepad. She spent most of her time in her room reading and drawing rather than spending time outside or playing like a six-year-old.

Mariam had warned Janet to never force Sanaa into doing what she didn't want to do and just give her space. Janet understood, but Sanaa was a kid. She needed to play and have a childhood like a normal kid. Janet just sighed and left the living room.

Since Sanaa was sleeping, Janet decided to go outside for some fresh air, at least for a few minutes. As she was walking to the front door, the sheikh came down the stairs.

"Good afternoon, sheikh," Janet greeted him.

"Afternoon," he replied. "Where is Sanaa?" he asked.

"She fell asleep in the living room." Janet smiled. Sanaa was so adorable.

"She fell asleep?" The sheikh looked surprised. Janet nodded.

"She was dozing off as she was watching TV. She was trying to fight it at first but then finally gave in."

"I see."

Just then, the living room door opened, and Sanaa walked out. She approached Janet quickly. "Oh, you've woken up," Janet said. Sanaa scribbled on her notepad and showed it to Janet.

Why did you let me sleep?

Janet gasped. "You were sleeping, so I left you to sleep in peace. You seemed tired," she said. Sanaa frowned at Janet before she stormed up the stairs. Janet was confused; what was wrong with letting her have a nap? She looked at the sheikh for an answer.

"She doesn't like taking naps in the afternoon," he explained. Janet gasped.

"She's a child; she needs naps," Janet said. The sheikh looked at her with a blank facial expression.

"Let her do what she wants." He opened the front door and walked out. Janet sighed. It was only day one on the job, and she had already upset Sanaa.

Chapter 4

Basil stepped out of the shower and towel-dried himself. He changed into a white T-shirt and a pair of khaki trousers. Sunday was really the only day he rested. He was used to working a lot because he wanted to expand his family business.

Basil headed downstairs for breakfast. He walked into the dining room and sat down. There was a newspaper on the table, as usual. He opened the newspaper and started reading it. Janet and Sanaa walked in moments later. Janet was wearing a pair of grey trousers and a blue camisole. Her hair was tied into a high ponytail. She had soft curly hair. Her appearance was smart, which pleased Basil.

"Good morning," Janet greeted Basil.

"Morning," he replied. Sanaa sat in the chair opposite him. "Did you sleep well?"

"I did, thank you," Janet replied. Basil and Sanaa both looked at her with their eyebrows raised. "What? Oh, you weren't asking me." Janet smiled awkwardly.

I slept fine, Sanaa wrote on her notepad. Basil nodded. The maids brought in trays of food and put them on the table.

"Shall I dish for you?" Janet offered Sanaa. Sanaa nodded, giving Janet the go-ahead. Janet picked up a serving spoon and put some scrambled eggs on Sanaa's plate. Basil watched Janet serving Sanaa. Janet promptly served the food and then poured orange juice in a glass for her. When she was finished, she looked up at the sheikh.

"Shall I dish for you too?" she offered.

"No." Basil folded the newspaper and placed it on the table.

"Okay," Janet replied. "I'll be in the kitchen if you need me, or do you prefer me to stay in here?"

"Do whatever you please."

"It's fine. I'm happy to do whatever makes you comfortable. When Sanaa is eating alone, I can stay in here, but if you're with her, I suppose it…"

"You talk too much."

Janet just stared at him with her jaw hanging open for a moment. "I'll be in the kitchen," she sulked. She turned on her heel and headed towards the kitchen. She pushed the brown doors and walked in. Basil was slightly amused by her reaction, but he didn't feel bad for what he had said. He liked peace at mealtimes, most of the time. He wasn't a big talker and found it uncomfortable to be around talkative people. He served breakfast for himself and started eating. Every morning, the maids prepared a buffet of breakfast foods. Every day, he ate the same thing: scrambled eggs, black coffee and fruit. However, he wanted his daughter to have a choice every day. No matter how small or large the matter, he wanted to provide everything for Sanaa, especially since her mother passed away.

It broke Basil's heart to see his daughter's demeanor change after her mother passed away. Sanaa stopped talking altogether. The doctors didn't find any injuries and said that it might have happened due to a big shock.

After they finished eating, the maids came in to clear the table. Janet came in for Sanaa. "What would like to do today?" she asked her. Sanaa shrugged her shoulders. Janet looked outside and then looked back at Sanaa. "Would you like to play outside?" she asked. Sanaa shook her head.

"Okay, we can go for a walk or…"

Sanaa wrote down: *I want to read.*

Janet nodded. "Alright, then, I guess I can do some laundry," she said. Sanaa stood up and waved at Basil before she walked out of the room. Basil rose to his feet.

"What do you normally do over the weekends?" Janet asked Basil.

"What?" Why was she asking him that? Why did she need to know how he spent his weekends? Her focus was Sanaa.

"Oh, I'm asking if you and Sanaa have something you like to do over the weekends usually."

"No."

"Oh?" She didn't seem content with Basil's answer. She smiled awkwardly. "I'll go and get started on the laundry." She turned and headed for the exit. Basil didn't say anything; he just watched her walking out of the room. He just shook his head and headed out of the room. Weekends were nothing special for him and Sanaa. He worked on most Saturdays, and on Sundays, he just wanted to read, watch the news, go horseback riding or for a drive.

Basil's wife was usually the one who spent much time with Sanaa. Now that she was gone, Sanaa didn't want to spend time with anyone and had just shut down. Sanaa had just lost the spark she used to have, and he didn't know how to fix it.

***

Janet dragged herself out of bed and went to have a shower. Waking up early in the morning was always hard for her; she hated mornings. If she could she would be happy to wake up at 10 a.m. or 11 a.m., but she had to be up early to take Sanaa to school.

The Sheikh's Second Chance

As she towel-dried herself, Janet hoped the week would go by smoothly. During the weekend, she had tried to talk to Sanaa and get to know her, but Sanaa wasn't opening up to her. It didn't help that the sheikh was a bit cold. Whenever Janet tried to speak to him, he barely spoke to her. It was a mission impossible to get a conversation going with him.

Janet wanted to wear a pair of jeans and a T-shirt, but Mariam had warned her that the sheikh wanted anyone working for him to dress smartly. So, she decided to wear a pair of black trousers and a white camisole and a black blazer. She finished her outfit with a pair of black shoes and then tied her hair up into a ponytail. She quickly made her bed and then headed out of the room.

The room Janet was staying in was down in the basement level of the house, where all the other housemaids had their rooms. Janet didn't mind; the room was beautiful. It was bigger than her room that she used to share with her sister before they fled Corpus Christi. This new room in the sheikh's house was furnished with a four-poster double bed, a dressing table and a closet. The bathroom was ensuite.

Janet headed out of the room, down the corridor and then up the stairs and through the door which connected the staircase to the corridor leading to the kitchen. She walked in and greeted the other maids and the chef. They were already awake and preparing breakfast for the sheikh. Janet left the kitchen through the dining room and then headed up the stairs. It was such a long trek from her bedroom to Sanaa's bedroom, Janet thought to herself.

Janet knocked on Sanaa's bedroom door before she walked in. She poked her head through. "It's me," Janet whispered. She walked in slowly. To Janet's surprise, Sanaa was already awake. She was in her bathrobe, and her hair was wet.

"Morning. Have you bathed already?" Janet was surprised. Sanaa nodded. "That's impressive. I have a six-year-old sister, and she doesn't bathe herself without being woken up and having her bath run for her."

Sanaa didn't respond; she just walked into her closet silently. Janet followed her into the massive walk-in closet, which was the size of a medium sized bedroom. It was incredible. It was arranged into three sections, one for clothes, one for coats and one for shoes and bags. Janet stood there in amazement. She was amazed by the closet and by how independent Sanaa was. She picked out her school uniform and then looked at Janet. She dismissed her with her hand.

"Oh, you want to change, but you want me to leave?" Janet asked. Saana nodded. "Okay." Janet turned on her heel and left the closet. She waited inside Sanaa's room while Sanaa was changing.

Sanaa emerged from the closet a few minutes later all dressed in her school uniform: a white round-collar blouse and a blue skirt with white tights. "Sit down; I'll do your hair," Janet said to Sanaa as she gestured towards the dressing table.

Sanaa nodded and went to sit down at the dressing table. Janet walked over and picked up a pink handle brush from the table. She opened the drawers in search of a blow-dryer. When she found it, she plugged it into the socket and turned it on. She brushed Sanaa's hair as she blow-dried it and made sure that it didn't get too hot. When it was dry, Janet parted it in the middle and then tied it into two buns.

"You look adorable," Janet said to Sanaa.

Sanaa stood up and went into her closet and retrieved a schoolbag. Then she and Janet headed downstairs for breakfast. Sanaa had breakfast by herself, according to the maids the sheikh had already left.

After breakfast, they headed out of the house. There was a black sedan waiting outside the house for Sanaa and Janet. The driver got out of the car and opened the backseat door. Sanaa climbed into the back and strapped her seatbelt on. Janet got in and sat next to her. "Thank you," she said to the driver. He nodded

The Sheikh's Second Chance

and shut the door behind her. The drive to Sanaa's school was about ten minutes.

"Shall I walk you inside?" Janet asked Sanaa. They had just parked outside the school. There were other cars parked, and parents were hugging and kissing their children.

Sanaa shook her head and got out of the car. "Have a nice day!" Janet shouted after Sanaa, but Sanaa didn't turn or wave. Janet felt sad for her, walking into school alone without a parent hugging or kissing her.

"Let's go," she said to the driver after Sanaa had disappeared into the building.

"Yes, ma'am," the driver replied. He was wearing a black suit and a white shirt. It was odd for Janet to be driven around in an expensive car. She had never even owned a car. She lived a very basic life.

Janet arrived back at the sheikh's house around 9 a.m. She had about six hours until she had to go back to pick up Sanaa. She was going to use that time to clean Sanaa's room, do her laundry and perhaps help the other maids with housework.

There was a black Range Rover parked at the front of the house. Janet eyed the car before she headed towards the front door. Suddenly the thick wood and glass front door swung open. Janet's eyes widened.

The Sheikh's Second Chance

"Oh, morning, sheikh," she greeted the sheikh as he walked out of the house with a folder in his hand. "I thought you had left for work already."

The sheikh knitted his eyebrows together as he walked past her. He was wearing a pair of black trousers and a navy-blue shirt. He smelled good, Janet thought to herself. She caught a whiff of his cologne as he walked past her.

"I just dropped Sanaa off at school," she said to him as she turned around and watched him walk away.

"Okay," he replied without turning around. He had a very broad back. Janet could see the outline of his muscles through his shirt. He had long, strong legs to support his muscular upper body.

The sheikh stopped walking and turned around, making eye contact with Janet. Her eyes flew wide open. She had been caught, staring. She just grinned and waved. She turned on her heel and opened the front door. She walked in quickly and shut the door behind her. "That was awkward," she mumbled to herself.

Chapter 5

Basil crossed his eyebrows as he watched Janet rushing into the house. He was amused by how Janet reacted to being caught staring at him. She had run into the house when Basil turned around. Basil shook his head and got into his Range Rover. He started the car engine and drove off.

He arrived at the office about fifteen minutes later. He parked at his spot, which was only reserved for him. He grabbed the folder from the passenger's seat and got out of the car.

"Morning, sheikh," the receptionist greeted him as he walked in.

"Morning," Basil replied. He walked through the turnstiles. He went into the elevator and headed up to the eighth floor. Basil headed to his office when the elevator doors opened.

"Morning, sheikh," Mariam greeted him as she rose from her seat.

"Any messages for me?" he asked as he walked past her and headed into his office. Mariam rushed in after him.

"Joshua Walters wants to set up a meeting with you. He'd like to buy oil from us. There was a call from

The Sheikh's Second Chance

Mike Sanders; he said the oil rig in Austin looks good, and he'll send in a report. And your mother called," said Mariam.

Basil sat down at his desk and looked up at Mariam. "My mother?" he asked.

"Yes," Mariam replied. Basil leaned back in his chair and sighed. "She said that you need to call her as soon as you get in."

Basil sighed. His mother had called his cell phone a few times. "I'll call her later," he said.

"How is it working out with Janet so far?"

"Who?"

"Sanaa's new nanny."

"Oh," Basil almost chuckled. "She talks too much."

"Normally, that's a good thing when dealing with children, but Sanaa is different," Mariam replied. Basil grunted in response. "We'll just have to see how she does," she continued.

"We'll see."

Mariam nodded before she headed out of Basil's office. Mariam had been Basil's secretary for over five years. She had proved herself to be very organized, resourceful, trustworthy and efficient.

Basil spent the rest of the day reviewing contracts and meeting with engineers and potential business partners. After finishing the work Basil left the office at 8 p.m. and headed home.

Janet was coming down the stairs when Basil walked through the front door. She was wearing a tracksuit and a T-shirt. Her shift was practically over since Sanaa would be in bed at that time. So, Basil couldn't complain about her clothes.

"Good evening, sheikh," she greeted him.

"Is Sanaa asleep?" he asked. Janet nodded.

"I just came back from checking on her."

"I see." Basil nodded. He headed to the dining room. Janet walked with him.

"Busy day?" she asked.

"As always." He was normally good at reading people, but he couldn't read Janet. He couldn't tell what kind of a person she was, other than a talkative person.

Ruth was in the dining room, setting up the dinner table, when Basil and Janet walked in. "Good evening, sheikh," she greeted him. "Dinner will be served in a few moments," she said before she disappeared into the kitchen.

"You often have dinner at this time?" Janet asked.

"Yes." He pulled out a chair and sat down at the table. "What did you do before you started working here?" He knew she worked at a shipping company, of course, because he had Mariam carry out a background check on her, but he wanted to find out more.

"I worked as a secretary at a shipping company," she replied.

"You went from that to being a nanny; it's a big change."

Janet laughed awkwardly. She was standing just a few feet away from Basil. "Yes, it is, but it's a good change," she replied. Basil raised an eyebrow.

"Why did you resign?" he asked.

"Um, my family and I had decided to leave town and start afresh somewhere. I also wanted a job in a different sector," she said. She laced her fingers together. She had medium length nails that were neatly shaped and clean.

"You said your family consisted of just your mother, your sister and yourself?" He remembered her talking about it during the interview. Janet nodded.

"Just the three of us. My mother never remarried after my father passed away," she replied. She had a soft voice. She cleared her throat. "I heard about your wife's passing, my condolences," she said.

"Don't," he said sternly.

"Sorry?" she looked up.

"Don't talk about my wife."

The Sheikh's Second Chance

"I, um, I don't mean to talk about her or anything. I just wanted to express my condolences."

"Your shift is finished; you're dismissed."

Janet's eyes widened. "I didn't mean to upset you," she said softly. She turned on her heel and headed towards the kitchen. Basil ran his hand through his hair. He didn't intend on snapping at her, but he didn't want to talk about his wife. Her untimely departure had left nothing but anguish.

Ruth walked in moments later with his dinner. She served him in silence before she disappeared back into the kitchen. That was how Basil liked to be served, in silence. Janet didn't seem to get it; she seemed always to have something to talk about. Basil picked up his fork and knife and started eating. He didn't want to be bothered by thoughts of Janet. She was probably not going to last long anyway.

***

Janet's phone rang, disturbing her from her sleep. She rubbed her eyes and grabbed the phone from the bedside table. She swiped the answer button. "Hi, Ma," she answered her phone.

"Hi, Janet, are you still sleeping?" her mother asked.

"Yes, it's Saturday."

"It's 9 a.m. though. You should be awake now."

The Sheikh's Second Chance

Janet yawned. "During the weekends, she calls me when she needs me. I don't have to wake her up or anything. So, I get more sleep today," she answered. Mariam had told her that her weekends were somewhat flexible. Janet didn't need to wake Sanaa up early. She only needed to attend to her if Sanaa asked or if she was going somewhere.

"How was your week?" Janet's mother asked.

"It was tough."

"How so?"

"Sanaa isn't warming up to me, and neither is the sheikh. The last time I spoke to him, I expressed my condolences, and he snapped at me."

Her mother sighed. "He's probably still hurting and doesn't want to talk about it," she said.

"Maybe, but I didn't mean anything bad."

"You have to talk to him only about his daughter. Keep your head down and don't get in his affairs."

"Ugh." Janet sat up. "This is harder than working for Pablo." When she worked for Pablo, she knew how to do her job, and he never complained. The hardest part of the job was knowing about his illegal affairs.

"Has he tried to contact you?"

"No, Mom, he can't. I changed my number, and we're hundreds of miles away from him. Don't worry; we're safe," she reassured her mother. She still worried about Pablo finding them. Janet felt as though she could relax a bit, now that it had been three months, and there had been no sightings of him. She had destroyed her old SIM card and thrown the phone away before they left Corpus Christi. There was no way for Pablo to track her or contact her.

"Okay," her mother replied.

"How's Kimmie?" Janet asked.

"She's fine; she misses you."

"I miss her too." Janet jumped out of bed. Since her ringing phone had woken her up, she decided to get out of bed. "Have you started looking for houses?"

"Not yet."

"Can you look for an affordable place we can rent? I'll send you money for a deposit and first month's rent when I get paid. It'd be better if you could live here in Dallas, then I can easily visit when I have time off," she said.

"Just focus on your job. I'm looking for a better paying job."

"No, I uprooted us from our home, and so it should be my responsibility to get us a new home. Besides, there's no one to look after Kimmie when you're working."

"I don't want to burden you."

The Sheikh's Second Chance

"You're not. Let me know when you've found something. I love you."

"It's temporary that I am without income. When Kim starts going to school again after the summer, I'll work while she's in school. I love you too," her mother said before she hung up.

Janet hated the situation she had caused. She just wanted her family to be happy and settled. She was grateful for the job that was paying well. She owed it to herself and her family to keep the job. To do that, she needed to stay on the sheikh's good side.

She went into the bathroom and had a quick shower. She changed into a pair of blue jeans and a white T-shirt. She then slipped into white sneakers and laced them up before heading upstairs. She was feeling quite hungry. She put her cell phone in her pocket and took her work phone with her just in case Sanaa messaged or called. She headed up the stairs and into the kitchen. She greeted the other maids and then asked them about Sanaa. They told her that she had her breakfast in bed. She wanted to watch cartoons in her room without getting disturbed.

Janet decided to message Sanaa. "Morning, Sanaa, hope you slept well. I'm going for a walk. Text or call if you need me."

Janet headed out of the house and went for a walk. The sheikh's estate was large. She didn't quite realize how large it was until she went on her walk. She climbed over the wooden fence and walked into what seemed like the woods. It was nice to be out, walking, enjoying the fresh air and just clearing her thoughts, Janet thought to herself. Suddenly she heard a hissing noise. She turned around and saw a snake slithering next to a big rock.

Janet's eyes widened, and then she started screaming. She had grown up in the city and had never encountered snakes. She didn't know what to do. She started taking a few steps back, but the snake slowly started slithering towards her. Her senses were dulled; she was struck by fear and wasn't sure what to do. She wanted to run, but she had heard that snakes moved faster than humans in the grass.

Suddenly she heard a loud galloping noise. "Take my hand," she heard. She turned her head and saw the sheikh on a huge black horse, extending his hand out to her. Janet didn't know where he was coming from, or that he owned a horse, and she had never been on a horse before, but she didn't care. She didn't want to be bitten by a snake. She took his hand, and he pulled her up onto the horse. He managed to pull her up with ease and set her on the horse, in front of him, with her legs to one side and her back to the other.

"Ya," the sheikh whipped the horse, and they galloped away.

Chapter 6

"Heee," the sheikh called out as he tugged on the reins. The horse slowed down and then came to a halt; they had arrived at the stables. Janet hadn't been at the stables yet; she hadn't even known that there were stables and so many horses.

The sheikh dismounted from the horse first and held his hand out to Janet. She placed her hand in his, and he helped her down from the horse. Much to her surprise, his hands were warm and soft; unlike his personality. He was cold and unfriendly. She didn't know if he was like that to everyone or just her.

"Thank you, sheikh," Janet said. Her heart was still pounding; she'd never liked snakes. They frightened her. "I don't know what I'd have done if you didn't arrive just then."

"What were you even doing there?" he asked, his face showing a hint of amusement.

"I just went out for a walk; I didn't think there would be snakes there. The thought didn't even cross my mind." Janet shivered. Basil gave half a smile before he grabbed the reins of the horse and pulled it into the stable. Janet raised her eyebrows. She'd never seen the sheikh smile or even laugh. Now here he was, amused, because of a scary situation she'd just faced.

"Are you laughing at me?" Janet asked the sheikh.

"It was an amusing sight, I must admit," he replied. He put the horse in a stall and closed and locked the stable gate.

"Of me screaming?"

Basil didn't answer; his smile only grew bigger.

"It was scary." Janet pouted. She couldn't believe that the sheikh was laughing at her. He turned to face her.

"It was a small snake and probably harmless," he said.

"It wasn't small."

Basil shook his head and started walking. Janet watched the sheikh walking past her. He looked much better when he smiled, she thought to herself. Janet started walking after the sheikh. She had to rush to catch up with him.

"Where is Sanaa?" he asked her.

"She's in her room. Ruth told me that she had breakfast in her room and didn't want to be disturbed. So, I sent her a text message letting her know I was going out for a walk. I must check up on her as soon as I get back in the house," Janet replied.

The sheikh sighed. "I see," he replied. He seemed slightly worried. Janet wanted to ask about his

The Sheikh's Second Chance

worries, but the last time she tried speaking to him about something personal, he snapped at her.

"She's so smart," Janet decided to talk about something positive. "I'm so impressed that she reads very well at such a young age."

"Yes, her teacher said she's at the reading level of a twelve-year-old."

Janet gasped. She knew that Sanaa was smart but not that smart. "That's amazing; you must be proud," she said. Even though it was amazing and impressive, she was still a child, and it saddened Janet to see her not play and smile like a child her age.

Janet rushed up to Sanaa's room when they arrived back at the house. She knocked on the door before she entered the room. Sanaa was sitting on her bed, drawing in her sketchbook.

"Hi." Janet smiled as she walked in. "I just wanted to check up on you."

Sanaa looked at Janet and then scribbled *I'm fine.* Janet smiled and nodded. She looked at the sketchbook. There were drawings of horses, clouds, the sky.

"Wow, that's beautiful," she said.

You can go, Sanaa wrote down.

"Are you sure you don't want company?" Janet asked her. Sanaa shook her head.

The Sheikh's Second Chance

"Okay. Call me if you need me." Janet waved at Sanaa before she walked out. As she shut the door, the sheikh was just about to enter his room, which was next to Sanaa's. He looked at Janet and raised his eyebrows as if to ask about Sanaa.

"I was just kicked out." Janet giggled.

"That doesn't surprise me." Basil gave half a smile before he entered his room.

Janet headed down to the laundry room, which was on the basement level of the house. There she ran into Ruth, one of the maids she had met before.

"Hi," Janet greeted her.

"Hello," Ruth replied.

Janet put Sanaa's clothes in the washing machine. "How are you?" she asked Ruth as she put in the detergent and then pushed the start button.

"I'm well, thank you," Ruth replied.

"How long have you worked for the sheikh?"

"Ten years."

Janet raised her eyebrows. "It's a long time," she said. Ruth responded with a nod. She was a woman of very few words.

"What happened to Sanaa's nanny, the one who worked here before me?" Janet asked.

"She was let go."

The Sheikh's Second Chance

"Fired?"

"Yes."

"Why?"

Ruth shut the other washing machine and pressed the start button after she had finished loading it up. "They all get fired," she said. Janet crossed her eyebrows.

"What do you mean?" she asked. Ruth sighed before she turned to face Janet. She was just a little bit taller and slimmer than Janet. Her dark hair was tied into a low bun. She had dark eyebrows that framed her face and complemented her dark almond complexion.

"Since the madam passed away, Sanaa has had many nannies. Each lasted no longer than two weeks. In the eyes of Sheikh El-Masry, no one is good enough to look after his daughter," Ruth explained.

"The madam, I mean his wife, she looked after Sanaa before she passed away?"

"Yes, she didn't work. She stayed home with Sanaa."

Janet sighed. Since Sanaa spent most of her time with her mother, it made sense that she wouldn't open up to her nannies.

***

Basil stood on the patio, staring into the distance. He had so much on his mind. It had been two weeks since Sanaa had a new nanny, and there was no change. Sanaa wasn't warming up to her. She was still shut down and not talking. It bothered Basil so much, he wanted a nanny that would be good to Sanaa, and that Sanaa would like and trust.

"Good evening, sheikh," Janet said as she walked out onto the patio and stood next to Basil.

"Evening," he replied.

"Are you alright? You look as though you have something on your mind."

"I do."

She moved a little bit closer to him. "Do you want to talk about it?" she asked. Basil raised an eyebrow and looked at her. He wondered why she was asking, it wasn't like he was going to tell her, and she knew that. Many times, he had told her to only focus on Sanaa.

"I guess not," she mumbled.

"What are you doing here?" he asked.

"Oh, yes, I wanted to ask you something." She played with her fingers and didn't say anything else for a moment.

"Hurry up and speak." Basil tended to be impatient.

"It's not a big deal, really. There's a carnival in town, can I take Sanaa there?"

The Sheikh's Second Chance

"No." There was no way he was going to allow his daughter to be in such an environment. There would be too many people; anything could happen.

"Oh, I thought it'd be fun." Janet sighed. "I'd like to do something nice for Sanaa."

"You're impulsive," he said to her. "My daughter's safety is a priority."

"I know, and I'd never do anything that would bring harm to her."

Basil shook his head. "No, I don't think you're the right fit for her," he said. Janet raised her eyebrows.

"What does that mean?" she asked him.

"It means that your services here are no longer required. Your pay will be transferred to your account; you can leave now."

"Because of the carnival?"

"Because you don't seem to understand her or her life. You always suggest peculiar things, and your focus doesn't seem to be on her. You're always trying to meddle into my business," Basil said calmly. Janet narrowed her gaze at him.

"I appreciate you having given me the job, but I can't leave without speaking my mind," she said. Basil leaned against the table and waited for her to speak.

"Sanaa is a child. She needs to do things that children do."

"Like?"

"Playing outside, eating junk food, going to carnivals and fairs." Janet threw her hands in the air. "I know that she lost her mother and…"

"Choose your words carefully," he warned.

"She shut down because of her mother's passing, and because of that, she needs stability. Changing nannies all the time isn't good for her. She needs…"

"If you have finished, you can leave now," Basil cut her off. He no longer wanted to listen to her. There was no way he was going to listen to someone else tell him what his child needed.

"Fine." Janet sighed. "Can I at least say goodbye to Sanaa before I leave?"

"No."

Janet's face dropped. She looked so disappointed. Could it be that she really cared about Sanaa? Basil wasn't sure and didn't care. Janet turned on her heel and left.

Basil couldn't believe Janet's little tantrum. Out of all the maids he had fired, she was the only one that dared to tell him off. Who did she think she was anyway? What gave her the right to speak about his daughter like this? She had only known Sanaa for two weeks. Basil shook his head and headed back into the house.

The Sheikh's Second Chance

As Basil was walking down the corridor, Janet walked out of the dining room with her suitcase. She stopped and looked at him. "Take care," she said. She pulled her suitcase as she headed out of the front door. Basil didn't try to stop her or say anything. He pulled his phone out of his pocket as he kept walking. He needed to call Mariam and let her know that she needed to find another nanny.

Just as he was about to head up the stairs, Basil saw Sanaa standing on the stairs looking at the front door. She was in a white dress and had her hair down. She had her notepad in her hands.

"Sanaa, are you okay?" he asked her.

Where is she going? she wrote down.

"You don't have to worry about her; I'll get you another nanny," he replied. Sanaa's eyes widened and started racing. "What's wrong?" Basil rushed up to her and held her shoulders. Her eyes welled up.

"Sanaa, what's wrong?" he asked her.

I want her, she wrote down. Basil raised his eyebrows.

"What?"

Call her back.

Chapter 7

Janet dragged her suitcase as she walked away from the sheikh's house. She couldn't believe that she had been fired after working there for only two weeks. She refused to accept the sheikh's reasons for firing her; he didn't like her, probably never did from the beginning. Janet stopped walking. Had she overstepped when she had spoken to the sheikh about Sanaa? she asked herself. Most parents never wanted to be told about their children and given advice by other people, especially from those that didn't have children. It was just that Janet was worried about Sanaa and she cared about her.

She started walking again and approached the large iron gates. The security guard opened the same side gate for her. "Thank you," she said to him. Just as she was about to walk out, she heard someone calling her name.

"Janet! Wait!" she heard. Janet crossed her eyebrows as she turned around. She saw Ruth rushing towards her.

"What's wrong?" Janet asked her.

"The sheikh asked me to call you back."

"Why?"

"I don't know; he just asked me to call you back promptly."

"Does he want to yell at me more?" Janet sighed. "Let's go find out," she added. Janet and Ruth walked up the long stone driveway and headed back up to the house. On the way back, Janet wondered why the sheikh had called her back. He had heartlessly fired her at 9 p.m. He didn't even wait until the morning, and he hadn't even allowed her to say goodbye to Sanaa.

Ruth opened the front door and walked in. Janet followed behind her. The sheikh and Sanaa were standing at the bottom of the stairs.

"Hey, sweetheart," Janet said to Sanaa. "I'm sorry for leaving without saying goodbye."

Sanaa walked towards Janet and held on to Janet's top and just looked at her. She had sadness in her eyes. Janet stroked her head. "What's wrong?" Janet asked softly. Ruth quickly walked off and headed towards the living room.

"Sanaa wants you to stay," said the sheikh. Janet looked at him and raised her eyebrows.

"Really?" Janet asked. The sheikh nodded.

"She doesn't want another nanny; she wants you."

Janet looked at Sanaa and then back at the sheikh. A smile tugged at the corner of her mouth. Less than twenty minutes before, the sheikh had told her that she wasn't good for Sanaa.

"Does that mean I'm not fired then?" Janet asked the sheikh.

"You can take your job back, with a 20 percent increase in your salary," he said.

"I see." Janet looked down at Sanaa who was still standing at her side. At that moment, the little girl looked up at Janet and smiled. It was the first time Janet had seen her smile, and it warmed her heart. Janet returned her smile.

"I think an apology is owed," Janet said as she looked up to the sheikh. He narrowed his gaze at her and grunted.

"I misjudged you." He turned on his heel and walked off. Janet smiled and shook her head.

"Let's get you to bed," Janet said to Sanaa as she took her hand. They both headed up the stairs and down the hallway.

Janet tucked Sanaa into bed. "I didn't know you liked me that much," Janet teased Sanaa.

Sanaa smiled and turned away, giving Janet her back. Janet giggled and stroked her head before she left. She headed back downstairs and retrieved her suitcase that she had left by the entrance. She went down to her bedroom and unpacked her stuff. What a crazy night it had been.

***

The next morning, Janet returned to the sheikh's house around 10 a.m. from dropping Sanaa off at school. She opened the front door and walked into the house. The sheikh was coming down the stairs. He was wearing a navy-blue suit; he looked and smelled good as always. He approached Janet and paused in front of her.

"Good morning, sheikh," she greeted him.

"Are you coming from dropping off Sanaa?" he asked.

"Yes," Janet nodded. The sheikh didn't say anything for a moment. He just stared at Janet. Him being that close to her and staring at her like that made her nervous. She wasn't sure what was on his mind. His gaze dropped to the ground.

"I was not good to her," said the sheikh. Janet crossed her eyebrows.

"Who?" she asked.

"My wife." Basil sighed. He looked up. "I didn't buy her flowers, take her out on dates or do any of those things normal married people do."

Janet wasn't sure what to say. She was shocked that the sheikh was talking to her about his wife.

The Sheikh's Second Chance

Whenever she had brought her up, he had snapped at her.

"We had an arranged marriage. I never courted her or anything like that. We just followed our parents' wishes and got married."

"I see," Janet replied plainly.

"I don't like talking about her because I wasn't good for her," he said.

"Did you ever hit her?"

"What? No."

"Did you emotionally abuse her?"

"No." The sheikh frowned. "What kind of man do you think I am?"

"If you've never done any of those things, then you shouldn't feel guilty," said Janet. The sheikh raised an eyebrow. "You both entered an arranged marriage, barely knowing each other. You couldn't be expected to be in love and be like normal couples. You're a sheikh and from a wealthy family. You grew up differently from others, don't blame yourself. All you can do now is be good to Sanaa," she added.

The sheikh didn't say anything. He smiled at Janet before he walked around her and headed out the door. Janet smiled to herself. He seemed much friendlier when he smiled, and more handsome too. It was a shame he didn't smile often. She also felt sad for him that he felt guilty about his wife passing without him being good to her. It was a guilt no one could fix since she had already passed away. There was nothing he could do for her. The only thing he could do was let it all go.

Janet headed into the kitchen for some breakfast. She normally ate after she had dropped Sanaa off. "Morning," she greeted Ruth as she walked in. Ruth was sitting at the kitchen table, eating her breakfast.

"Morning," Ruth replied. Janet retrieved her plate from the microwave and went to join Ruth at the table. "What happened last night?" Ruth asked her.

Janet shrugged her shoulders. "The sheikh fired me, then rehired me," she replied before she started eating. Ruth raised her eyebrows.

"That's unlike the sheikh, to go back on his decision."

"Apparently it wasn't his decision." Janet smiled.

"You're very lucky. Not many others get their jobs back."

Chapter 8

"Good morning, sheikh," Basil's employees greeted him as he entered the conference room. Mariam walked in after him and closed the door.

"Morning," he replied as he sat at the head of the table. "Shall we begin?"

"Yes, sheikh," Mariam replied. She switched on the projector and began her presentation. She was reporting the company's progress within the last month, its profits and losses. Basil found himself unable to concentrate on what she was saying. He found himself thinking about his earlier conversation with Janet.

To his surprise, he had spoken to her about his late wife. The words had left his mouth before he could stop them. Strangely enough, her words had brought him comfort. She wasn't as bad as Basil had thought. His daughter had even warmed up to her. He was still surprised that Sanaa didn't want to lose Janet. She had looked so distressed when she found out that Basil had fired Janet.

"What do you think, sheikh?" Mariam asked.

"What?" Basil hadn't heard anything Mariam had been saying. His thoughts were filled with Janet, annoyingly.

"We need to increase the amount of oil we import," said Mariam.

"Okay, send me a detailed report of the idea. I want to know if we have enough staff to handle the workload, how much profit it'll give us, everything." Basil rose to his feet. "Meeting adjourned."

"Yes, sheikh," Mariam replied.

Basil headed out of the conference room and returned to his office. He sat down in his leather chair as soon as he got into his office. Mariam walked in a few moments later. She closed the door behind her and approached his desk.

"Is everything okay?" she asked.

"Fine, why?" Basil leaned back into his chair. Mariam stood in front of him, dressed in black, posture straight and expression stern.

"You seemed a bit distracted during the meeting."

"Oh, it's nothing." Basil crossed his hands over his chest.

"Okay. You have a meeting at 12:30 with Brodo Petrols and a business call at 2:30," Mariam said to him.

"Alright," he said. Mariam nodded before she walked out of his office.

The Sheikh's Second Chance

***

Basil arrived at home just after 8 p.m. He had had a long and busy day at work, as usual. He unbuttoned his shirt as he walked into the dining room, with his blazer in the other hand. He asked one of the maids to make him a smoothie instead of a full dinner, as he didn't have much of an appetite.

When the smoothie was ready, he headed towards the patio for some fresh air. He often took walks at night; it helped to clear his mind. He pushed the doors open and stepped out into the cool night. He saw Janet sitting down in one of the chairs. She was wearing a loose-fitting white sweater and black slacks. Her hair wasn't tied back.

"What are you doing out here?" he asked. She gasped and placed her hand on her chest. She turned her head towards him.

"You frightened me," she replied.

"That wasn't my intention." He pulled out a chair and sat down.

"I just came out for some fresh air."

"I see." He took a sip of his smoothie.

"Sanaa is already sleeping. Today, she fell asleep quite early. I think she was tired," said Janet.

"I'll check on her when I go upstairs," he replied. Janet looked at his smoothie.

"Is that your dinner or just an after-dinner snack?"

"I don't have an appetite."

"Ah." Janet nodded. "Kim, my little sister, loves smoothies. She calls them sthmoothies." Janet laughed.

"She has a lisp?"

"Yes, it's so adorable. I miss her a lot."

There was silence between them for a moment. Basil drank his smoothie and just enjoyed the peace. He liked being still, especially at night, with the cool air and the moonlight.

"It's nice out here," said Janet as she looked up to the sky. "There are so many stars. Do you know anything about stars?"

"No," he answered. He didn't know about stars, nor did he want to. He didn't even want to talk about them, but it seemed as though Janet could talk about anything.

"Neither do I. I don't know how people know which star is which and all that big dipping stuff," she replied.

"Big dipping?" Basil raised an eyebrow, trying not to laugh.

"Yeah, you've never heard of them?" She gasped as she turned her head to look at him.

The Sheikh's Second Chance

"I'm sure that's not what it's called."

"It is! I'm sure it is."

"Okay," Basil said, knowing that she was wrong. There was no such thing as big dipping. He knew what she was trying to say. He just shook his head and drank a bit more of his smoothie.

"Oh, you don't believe me." Janet pulled out her phone from her pocket and started doing something. Basil could see her fingers at work from the corner of his eye. He didn't want to ask what she was doing. He just wanted to sit there in peace.

"Oh, it's Big Dipper." She laughed a little and tucked a lock of hair behind her ear. She had an adorable laugh. "I was close though," she added. Basil took a sip of his smoothie.

"You looked that up on the internet," he said.

"I had to; you didn't believe me."

"And I was right not to."

"Ha." Janet crossed her arms over her chest and looked away. The wind brushed her hair back and revealed her face to Basil. She was beautiful, he thought to himself.

"Sanaa's birthday is coming up," said Basil. Since she just kept on talking, he thought he'd talk to her about Sanaa's birthday.

"Aww really?" Janet asked. "When?"

"In two weeks."

"Are you going to throw her a party?"

"No, should I?"

"Well, what did you have planned?"

"Nothing." Basil shrugged his shoulders. "What do you do for a seven-year-old?"

"Throw her a party with clowns and jumping castles or take her to Disneyland. There's so much you can do for her."

"I don't know; she's not keen on people since her mother's passing."

"Okay, perhaps something intimate."

"I have no ideas." Basil rose to his feet.

"I'll think of something. Don't worry; I got your back."

Basil smiled to himself and headed inside the house. *I got your back,* she said. No one had ever said that to him. It made him smile and feel warm on the inside.

Chapter 9

Janet watched the sheikh walking away for a moment. She sighed as she looked away from him and just looked at the stars. The sheikh was such a complex man, she thought to herself. At face value, he was cold and aloof. However, Janet was starting to see a different side of him. There was a certain softness within him when he spoke about Sanaa and his wife. Janet was surprised when he had spoken to her about his wife's passing. He opened up about his guilt towards his wife. He went from snapping at her to confiding in her.

The breeze felt cold against Janet's skin. She got up from her seat and quickly headed down to her room. She changed into her pajamas and got into bed. She decided to call her mother before she went to sleep.

"Hello," her little sister answered the phone instead.

"Kimmie!" Janet was so excited to hear her sister's voice. "How are you, my darling?"

"I misth you," she said. Kim had a little bit of a lisp, and Janet thought it was adorable. Hearing her sister's voice made her smile.

"I miss you too."

"When will I sthee you?"

The Sheikh's Second Chance

"Soon, Kimmie."

"One of my teeth isth wobbly. Ma saysth it'll fall out soon." There was so much excitement in her voice.

"Really? The baby teeth are coming out, you're becoming a big girl," said Janet. Kim giggled in response.

"Is that Janet?" Janet heard her mother's voice in the background.

"Yesth," Kim replied.

"Hello," her mother came onto the phone.

"Hi, Ma," Janet greeted her.

"Hi, Janet, how are you?"

"I'm fine. I just miss you guys."

"We miss you too. How's the job?"

Janet sighed before she replied. "Interesting," she said.

"Why?" her mother asked.

"Sanaa is now warming up to me." Janet hesitated before she replied.

"What happened?"

"Huh, nothing. How's the house hunting going?"

"Don't try to change the subject; tell me what happened."

Janet didn't want to tell her mother that the sheikh had fired her because she didn't want her mother to worry. Unfortunately, her mother was already onto her. She already knew that there was something wrong.

"Um, I got fired," she said after a long pause.

"What?" her mother spat out.

"It's okay; I got rehired. Don't worry; I didn't do anything wrong."

"Then why were you fired?"

Janet explained to her mother what happened between her and the sheikh on the patio before he fired her and how he rehired her.

"That's a lot to take in," said her mother. "You haven't even worked there for a month, and all of that has happened."

Janet laughed. "I know it's crazy, but it's alright. The job isn't so bad, Sanaa is warming up to me, and the sheikh isn't so cold towards me anymore."

"He sounds like a hard man to please."

"He is."

Her mother sighed. "Just behave yourself and be careful. If you get fired again, I'm sure this time will be the last. There won't be any rehiring," she said.

"I agree. Alright, Ma, I'm in bed now. I'll speak to you later."

"Okay, baby girl."

Janet hung up the phone and put it on the nightstand. She switched the lights off and then went to bed.

***

Later that week, on Friday, Janet went to pick up Sanaa after a half-day at school. Janet was waiting for Sanaa in the car when she saw her walking out of the building. She paused at the school gates and looked at the other kids running into their parents' arms. She looked a little bit sad. Janet got out of the car.

"Sanaa!" she called out. Sanaa turned her head when she heard Janet calling her name. Janet smiled and waved at her. Sanaa held onto her bag straps and walked towards Janet.

"Hi." Janet stroked Sanaa's head and touched her shoulders. "How was your day?" she asked.

Sanaa shrugged her shoulders. She walked around Janet and opened the car door and hopped into the backseat. Janet got into the car after her.

"Let's go," Janet said to the driver.

"Yes, ma'am," he replied. He started the car engine and drove off. Sanaa didn't say anything on the way home. She just sat there quietly, staring out of the window.

They arrived back at the sheikh's house not too long after. Sanaa and Janet got out of the car and headed into the house. Sanaa went upstairs to get changed, and Janet went to the kitchen to fetch her lunch. She brought her plate into the dining room and prepared the table. When she was finished setting the table, Sanaa walked in. She had changed into a yellow summer dress.

"Perfect timing," Janet said to her.

Sanaa hopped into one of the chairs. She picked up her spoon and started eating her lunch. Janet joined Sanaa at the table and just watched her eating. She was playing with her food and eating slowly.

"What's wrong?" Janet asked Sanaa. Her mood had been off since Janet had picked her up from school. Sanaa shrugged her shoulders and put her fork down. She got off the chair and ran out of the room.

"Sanaa!" Janet called out after her. She stood up and followed her out.

Janet found Sanaa in her room, sitting on her bed, playing with her fingers. She looked so sad; it broke Janet's heart.

"Can I have a seat?" Janet asked her. Sanaa just shrugged her shoulders. Janet sat down next to Sanaa. "I noticed you've been a bit sad since after school.

The Sheikh's Second Chance

Was it because of the other kids hugging their parents? Do you miss your mom?" she asked.

"Yes," Sanaa said quietly. Janet's eyes flew wide open as she heard Sanaa speak for the first time. Her voice was so soft.

"Did you just speak? You did, didn't you?" Janet gasped. Sanaa looked at her and shook her head. Janet held Sanaa's little face in her hands. "It's okay; you can talk to me," she said gently. Tears streamed down Sanaa's face. Janet pulled Sanaa into her arms and wrapped her arms around her. She rubbed her back as she cried in her arms.

Sanaa cried for a while. It was obvious to Janet that she had been holding back for so long. It wasn't good for a child to suppress feelings like that. Janet rubbed her back and just let Sanaa cry it out.

Sanaa pulled out of Janet's embrace and looked up at her. "I miss mama," she said.

"I bet you do, sweetheart." Janet wiped the tears off her face. Sanaa sniffed a few times. With each sniff, her shoulders hunched up. "What happened that day?" Janet asked softly. Sanaa shook her head. It was clear that she wasn't ready to talk about it.

"It's okay; we don't have to talk about it." Janet hugged Sanaa. She wasn't surprised that Sanaa didn't tell her about what happened the day her mother

The Sheikh's Second Chance

died. She hadn't spoken to her father about it. Obviously, she wouldn't talk to Janet about it.

After a while, Sanaa fell asleep. Janet laid her down on the bed and covered her with the duvet. She walked out of the room and went downstairs. She busied herself with ironing Sanaa's clothes. As she was folding and organizing the clothes, she thought about Sanaa. It was great that she had decided to speak. It showed that she was starting to heal.

When Janet was finished ironing, she took the clothes upstairs to Sanaa's bedroom. When she walked in, Sanaa was still sleeping. It had been an hour and a half since she fell asleep. Janet didn't want to wake her up, so she put the clothes in the closet quietly and then left quickly. She closed the door quietly and then headed downstairs.

Janet saw Ruth coming from the dining room with a jar of water and a glass on a small tray. Janet looked at the tray and then raised an eyebrow.

"It's for the sheikh," she said. Janet's eyes widened.

"He's here?" she asked. He was early, she thought to herself. It was almost five o'clock, and he usually came home around 8 p.m.

"Yes, in his office."

"Okay, let me take the water to him."

"Ah…" Ruth looked unsure.

The Sheikh's Second Chance

"It's okay; I just need to speak to him." Janet stretched her arms out.

"Okay." Ruth handed the tray to Janet.

"Thanks." Janet took the tray and headed down the corridor. She walked past the living room and took a left turn just before she reached the doors leading to the patio. The sheikh's office was just at the end of that short corridor. Janet knocked on the door.

"Come in," the sheikh answered. Janet turned the door handle and then walked into the office. The sheikh was at the edge of the desk with a tablet in his hand. He was staring at it with his eyebrows knitted together.

"You're home early," said Janet.

"You brought the water," he said plainly.

"Yes, because…"

"You can just put it down on the desk and go," he cut her off. Janet began to walk towards him.

"I need to talk to you," she said as she approached him.

"Now isn't a good time."

Janet put the tray down. "It's important," she said gently.

"Janet, not now!" he snapped. He looked up from his tablet. He seldom called her by her name.

The Sheikh's Second Chance

"Sanaa spoke to me," she called out. She didn't know what was going on with the sheikh, it was clear that he wasn't in a good mood, but she didn't care. What she had to tell him concerned his daughter; it was more important than anything he had going on.

"What are you talking about?" The sheikh looked confused.

"Basil, Sanaa spoke to me. Not by writing stuff down, she actually spoke," Janet explained. "I heard her small soft voice."

Chapter 10

Basil put his tablet down so that he could focus on what Janet was saying. He hoped that she was not lying to him.

"You're telling me that my daughter, who hasn't spoken a word since her mother died, decided to speak now, and to you?" said Basil. He ignored the fact that she had just addressed him by his name and not as *sheikh*.

"Yes, I was so shocked."

"Why did she start speaking to you?"

"When I went to pick her up after school, I noticed her watching other children hugging their mothers. She looked quite sad, and since we got home, she was just sad and wasn't even eating."

Basil closed his eyes and shook his head. It broke his heart to know that his daughter was sad. He was prepared to give her everything in the world to make her happy. He wished he could give her back her mother, but that was the one thing he couldn't give her.

"She barely finished her lunch and just ran upstairs. I followed her and asked what was wrong. She told me that she missed her mama and started crying," said Janet.

"She cried?" Basil asked.

"Yes." Janet nodded. "A lot, for a while."

"My baby girl." Basil felt so sad that it wasn't him that his daughter had decided to speak to. It had been almost five months since she had stopped talking. He had always thought that if she started speaking, it would be to him.

"She's asleep now. She wore herself out crying."

Basil sighed. "What am I supposed to do now? Talk to her about it or not say anything?" he asked her. Basil didn't know what to do with Sanaa. He didn't have the right words to make her pain melt away.

"Talk to her," Janet said softly.

"And say what?" Basil raised an eyebrow.

"Let her know that you're here for her, hug her, kiss her."

She spoke as if it was easy. Maybe for her, it was easy, but for Basil, it wasn't. Emotions, hugs, kisses, Basil wasn't good with those kinds of things. He was good at gas and oil engineering and at running a business.

Janet smiled and touched his arm. "It's good that she's starting to talk again. Don't worry too much; it's going to be okay," she said, then turned on her heel and headed out. She paused in the doorway and looked at him.

"I'm sorry I came in here rudely, I just thought it was important that you knew." She smiled and headed out of the room.

It was strange how Janet's smiling used to annoy Basil; she was always talking too much and smiling too much. He couldn't take her seriously. Now her smiling made him feel better. After talking to her and having her smile at him and tell him that everything was going to be okay, he felt hope.

Basil sat down at his desk and switched on the computer. He had come home early because he had an important document in his home office that he needed to review before an important business trip he was going on the next day.

After a while, Basil checked his watch; it was 5:40. Sanaa must be awake now, he thought to himself. He stood up and walked out of the office and headed down the corridor. As he approached the living room, he heard the TV on. He went over to see if Sanaa was in there, and she was.

Sanaa was sitting on the sofa, leaning against Janet, with her elbow on her thigh. The two of them were sitting so comfortably and were so focused on whatever they were watching on the TV. He just stood in the doorway and watched them for a moment. It warmed his heart, just seeing his daughter like that. She was smiling; it had been a while since he had seen her smile.

Janet turned her head and saw Basil standing in the doorway. She smiled at him and nudged Sanaa.

"Hi, Sanaa," Basil greeted his daughter. Janet narrowed her gaze at him before she burst out laughing.

"You're so awkward," she mumbled. Basil rubbed the back of his neck; he was going to let that comment slide. How could his employee laugh at him so easily like that? he wondered. She was a bit cheeky at times.

Janet whispered something in Sanaa's ear. Sanaa looked up at Janet, and they both smiled at each other. Sanaa got off the sofa and walked over to Basil. She gestured for him to come closer. Basil crouched down in front of her. She wrapped her arms around him and placed a small soft face against his. Basil wrapped an arm around her and held her tightly.

It was such a nice feeling to be able to hold his daughter in his arms. He kissed her on the cheek and ran his hand through her hair. So many emotions coursed through him, happiness, sadness, grief, guilt.

One of the maids walked into the room. "I'm sorry to interrupt. I just wanted to let you know that dinner is ready," she said. Basil wasn't bothered by the maid's interruption because he wasn't sure what to do after hugging Sanaa, or what to say.

"Okay," Basil replied. The maid quickly exited the room. Sanaa pulled out of Basil's embrace.

"Can Janet have dinner with us?" she asked him. Basil narrowed his gaze at her.

"The first time you speak to me in a long time, and it's about Janet." Basil rose to his feet.

"Jealous?" Janet grinned at him.

"Let's go," he said to Janet.

Sanaa giggled and rushed to Janet's side. She took her hand, and the three of them walked through the adjoining door at the right corner of the room and walked into the dining room. There was a maid in there setting the table.

"Set a place for Janet," Basil instructed the maid.

"Yes, sheikh," she replied. She headed into the kitchen to retrieve more cutlery. Basil sat at the head of the table. Sanaa sat at his right side and Janet at his left. The maids brought in the food and served them swiftly.

As they started eating, Basil watched Sanaa for a moment. Her mood had changed completely; it was amazing. Then he looked over to his left, there was Janet, sitting there eating. It was the first time he had ever eaten a meal with her. It was odd, he thought to himself. Basil picked up his fork and started eating.

"I like it when you come home early," said Sanaa. It was lovely to hear her voice once again.

"You do?" Basil asked her. She nodded.

"We get to eat together."

"I agree with Sanaa; you should always come home early," said Janet. Basil raised an eyebrow at her. His work kept him so busy. It required him to work long hours to make sure that everything went smoothly. Basil didn't want his business to fail, not even slightly. However, he felt guilty about not spending enough time with Sanaa. He was the only parent she had left, and he needed to do better.

"I'm going to read," Sanaa said after they were finished eating.

"Are you sure? Don't you want to watch movies and eat junk food?" Janet wiggled her eyebrows.

"Don't be a bad influence," he said to her. "Sanaa, keep your routine. Self-discipline is important for success."

Janet crossed her eyebrows. "She's six," she said.

"And?"

"You're talking to a six-year-old about self-discipline." She narrowed her gaze at him. Basil slipped his hands in his pockets and shrugged his

The Sheikh's Second Chance

shoulders. He didn't think there was anything wrong with what he had said. Sanaa giggled and walked out of the room.

"It's amazing that she's talking again," Basil said after Sanaa had left the dining room.

"It really is." Janet smiled.

"I'm going on a business trip tomorrow," he said to Janet.

"Oh, are you? For how long?"

"A week."

"That's a long time. Where are you going?"

"Mexico, Canada and Egypt." Basil's company had branches in those three countries. He was going on the trip to oversee how things were going and to meet with a few clients. It was normal for him to go on a trip for a week. The timing was horrible because of Sanaa's upcoming birthday. "I'm telling you because I need you to handle preparations for Sanaa's birthday," he said.

"Oh, I can do that," she said. "But you will be back in time, right?"

"Yes." Basil fished his wallet out of his pocket and opened it. He took out a bank card and gave it to Janet. "Use this to buy anything you need for the party. There's no limit on it," he said. Janet took the card and put it in her pocket.

"Okay, we'll go wild, since there's no limit!" She wiggled her eyebrows. Basil stared at her with a blank look on his face. "It's a joke," she added.

He checked his watch. "I guess your shift has ended now," he said.

"Yes," she replied.

"What do you do with your evenings anyway?"

"Relax, sleep, catch up on TV shows, call my family."

"Nothing then."

Janet shrugged her shoulders. "That's what you're meant to do with your time off," she said.

"I see." Basil didn't know what to say next. He expected Janet to say something, but she didn't. They just stood there, in silence, staring at each other. She had nicely shaped eyebrows and brown eyes. Her lightly tanned skin was smooth, with a silky glow it. Her face was oval shaped. She had a perfect jawline and medium sized lips. Janet was really beautiful.

"Um, I'm going to bed." She laughed awkwardly as she turned on her heel and headed towards the kitchen and disappeared.

Chapter 11

A week had passed since Sanaa had started speaking. Even though she was now speaking, she only spoke to Janet and the sheikh. She still didn't want to talk to others. It was taking her a while to warm up to others. Janet went to pick up Sanaa after school.

Janet waited outside the school until Sanaa came out. When she saw her, she smiled and waved. Sanaa smiled and started running towards Janet when she saw her. She ran straight into her arms.

"Hey, sweetheart," Janet greeted her. "You seem to be in a really good mood today." She stroked her hair.

"I am!"

"Why?"

"We're on summer vacation now! And it's my birthday tomorrow," she said with so much excitement.

"It's your birthday tomorrow? Really? I didn't know," Janet joked.

"Yes, you did!" Sanaa giggled. The two of them climbed into the backseat of the car.

"Let's go for ice cream," said Janet.

"I like ice cream." Sanaa giggled. She looked excited.

The Sheikh's Second Chance

The driver drove off and headed into town. He parked outside the ice cream parlor. Janet and Sanaa got out of the car and quickly went into the shop. "What would you like?" Janet asked Sanaa. The shop served a range of flavors and different desserts.

"I want vanilla ice cream with chocolate sprinkles and macaroons and marshmallows," she said.

"That's a weird mix; you don't want to get a tummy ache," Janet replied as she laughed softly.

"No, I won't." Sanaa giggled.

Janet used the card the sheikh had left her to buy ice cream for Sanaa and herself. They went to sit outside the shop and started eating their ice cream. Janet had gotten cookies and cream flavored ice cream.

"I used to eat ice cream with mama," said Sanaa. Janet looked at her. "She liked eating macaroons with ice cream."

"Did she?" Janet smiled. Sanaa put her ice cream down on the table.

"I was with her."

"You were with her, when?"

"When she died." Sanaa had so much sadness in her eyes as she spoke. "There was so much blood." Tears rolled down her cheeks.

"You poor thing."

The Sheikh's Second Chance

Sanaa started sniffling and trying to fight the tears, but she was losing. Janet pulled Sanaa into her arms and gently stroked her back. It was sad for her to see Sanaa like that. Though Sanaa was starting to talk about her mother's death, it was tough for her. Janet could see her struggling to talk about it. She figured that Sanaa was traumatized by her mother's death, and that was why she stopped speaking.

"Let's go home," Janet said. She picked up Sanaa and carried her back to the car. As she was walking to the car, she noticed a brown-skinned man dressed in black, smoking and leaning against a black Camaro in the parking lot. The man looked up and stared at Janet. His dark gaze made her shiver. He watched her walking to the car, it made her nervous.

Janet opened the backseat car door and put Sanaa in the car first. She buckled the seatbelt and then walked around the car and got in from the other side. The driver got the car engine started and drove off.

As they were turning into the road that led to the sheikh's house, Janet noticed a black Camaro behind them. The car was behind them until they almost reached the sheikh's house and finally drove past them. Janet wondered if they were followed.

The security guard opened the gate for them when they arrived at the sheikh's house. They drove up the long driveway and parked just outside the house. Sanaa and Janet got out of the car and got into the house. While Sanaa went up to her room to get changed out of her uniform, Janet went to talk to Ruth.

"Is the sheikh back yet?" she asked her.

"No, are you waiting for him?" Ruth asked.

"Yeah," Janet nodded.

"Don't go down that road; it won't be good for you."

"Huh, what road?"

"You and the sheikh."

Janet raised an eyebrow. "Me and the sheikh?" She let out a laugh. "I don't have any feelings for him or anything like that. I'm only waiting for him to come back because it's Sanaa's birthday tomorrow," Janet explained.

"Okay." Ruth didn't sound convinced.

"Why wouldn't it end well anyway?" Janet was curious why she'd said that.

"In the time I have worked for the sheikh, many women have tried to gain his attention, they all failed." Ruth stared at Janet with a stern face. "He's not interested in fruitless dalliances."

"Neither am I," Janet replied. "I never once thought about starting a relationship with the sheikh. I don't want to lose my job; I have a family to look after."

"Alright. I'm just looking out for you." She turned on her heel and walked away. Janet crossed her eyebrows. Ruth was a peculiar one. They had talked on many occasions, but it never felt like they were getting any closer.

***

Most of Sanaa's friends had arrived and were already playing in the backyard. Janet had hired a company to set up a carnival in the sheikh's backyard. She thought it would be a fun idea for Sanaa's birthday.

Janet rushed upstairs to help Sanaa get ready for the party. "Right, let's get you dolled up," Janet said to Sanaa as she walked into her room.

"It's my birthday!" Sanaa screamed.

"Yes, it is." Janet giggled. She helped Sanaa get changed into a white dress and pink shoes. Janet curled Sanaa's hair and put ribbons in it. When they had finished getting ready, they headed downstairs.

The front door opened, and the sheikh walked in. "Daddy!" Sanaa screamed as she ran towards her father. The sheikh crouched down and embraced her.

"Happy birthday, habibti," he said.

"Thank you." Sanaa pulled out of his embrace. "Let's go," she said.

"Okay." The sheikh looked at Janet and mouthed *where is the party?*

The Sheikh's Second Chance

Outside, Janet mouthed back.

The three of them headed to the backyard through the patio. The backyard was beautifully arranged. There were different booths for different activities. There was a hotdog stand, a cotton candy stand, and a popcorn stand. There were juggling clowns, clowns on stilts and a jumping castle.

"Wow! It looks amazing!" Sanaa gasped. She looked at the sheikh. "Thank you, Daddy," she said to him before she ran off to join her friends. Janet and the sheikh were left standing together at the patio.

"You did all this?" he asked her.

"Yes, what do you think?" Janet asked him.

"I'd have never thought of that." He looked at Janet. "Thank you," he said to her.

"You're welcome, but I didn't do it alone. I had help from Ruth. She helped me run background checks on everyone that was coming to work here." She smiled. The sheikh smiled back.

"You're learning fast," he replied.

"I'm glad you got here on time. I was worried that you weren't going to make it."

The sheikh raised an eyebrow. "Worried for yourself or Sanaa?" he asked.

"Sanaa, of course," Janet protested. What was he trying to suggest? "How was your trip?" she asked.

The Sheikh's Second Chance

"Productive." The sheikh slipped his hands in his pockets and watched the kids running around and enjoying themselves. "What happened when I was gone?"

"Nothing out of the ordinary happened. Sanaa and I were just fine." Janet laced her fingers together.

"Good."

The children played on the jumping castle, they watched the clowns performing, and they ate hot dogs and cheeseburgers. Janet helped to look after the kids. She served them food and played with them. The sheikh kept his distance from the entire party. He sat on the patio and watched from a distance.

Janet checked the time; it was already past two, and it was time for the cake. She asked one of the maids to go retrieve the cake from the kitchen while she gathered everyone. She walked up to the patio to call the sheikh.

"You're antisocial," she said to him. The sheikh raised an eyebrow at her.

"You expected me to play with the kids?" he asked.

"Yes, I did."

"I saw." He narrowed his gaze at her. Janet started laughing.

"And there's nothing wrong with it, and I had fun."

"I'm not judging." He smiled a little.

"Yes, you are." Janet shook her head. "Anyway, I came here to call you over. It's time to cut the cake."

"I have to be there?" the sheikh asked.

"Yes, and you have to sing." Janet raised an eyebrow. "I will drag you there if I have to," she added. The sheikh raised his eyebrows, but just as he opened his mouth to say something, one of the maids walked out of the house with the cake.

"Happy birthday to you!" Janet started singing. She turned on her heel and walked with the maid towards the children. Everyone joined in and sang for Sanaa. The sheikh followed behind Janet and stood next to her.

"Make a wish!" she said to Sanaa.

"Okay." Sanaa closed her eyes and made her wish. She then blew out the candles. Everyone cheered her on and clapped their hands. Janet took the knife and helped Sanaa cut the first slice.

"You get to eat the cake first," Janet said. She smiled at Sanaa and stroked her rosy cheeks. Sanaa grinned and took a fork to taste her cake. Janet cut the next slice and handed to the sheikh.

"Thank you," he said to her.

"Is it enough, or shall I give you more?"

"Thank you for throwing this party for my baby. I haven't seen her this happy in a while."

The Sheikh's Second Chance

Janet rubbed the sheikh's arm. "It's fine; I like seeing her happy," she said. The sheikh stared at her for a moment before he smiled. His gaze made her insides melt. Janet tucked a lock of hair behind her ear shyly and looked down.

"Janet, have some cake." Sanaa approached Janet with a slice of cake, interrupting Janet's moment with the sheikh.

"Oh, thank you." Janet took the cake and started eating.

The rest of the party went well. The kids played and ate. Their parents picked them up around 5 p.m. After that, Sanaa went to her room and fell asleep. She was so tired from all the running and jumping around with her friends. Janet also went down to her room and threw herself onto the bed. She was tired too.

Chapter 12

Janet opened her eyes when she heard a knock on her door. She checked the time; it was only 8 a.m. Who was looking for her at 8 a.m. on a Sunday? she wondered. If it were important, they'd call her. Before she could decide on answering or ignoring, the door opened slowly, and a small head poked through.

"Sanaa!" Janet cried out. She was shocked to see her coming to her room at such an early time. "What are you doing here?" she asked.

"I just woke up." Sanaa rubbed her eyes. She was still wearing her nightgown. She walked over to Janet and climbed into bed with her.

"What's happening right now?" Janet laughed. Sanaa lay down next to her and looked at her.

"The party was so fun yesterday! I've never been to a carnival before."

"Really? Well, I'm glad you enjoyed it."

"This is the first birthday without mama."

"Aww, sweetheart." Janet stroked Sanaa's hair.

"We were going for lunch at some fancy hotel on Sunday, we had a reversation or something."

"A reservation?" Janet smiled. Sanaa was so adorable.

"Yeah. Daddy couldn't make it, so only me and mama went," she replied. Janet wasn't sure what Sanaa was talking about, but since it was about her mother, she wasn't going to interrupt. "A truck just hit us." Sanaa's lip started quivering.

"You don't have to tell me if you're not ready." Janet stroked Sanaa's cheeks.

"I want you to tell you." Sanaa wiped a tear from her eye. "Our car fell, and mama hit her head. So much glass poked her. There was blood everywhere." Sanaa started crying. Janet comforted her. She had lost her father years ago, but she was fortunate not to see him die the way Sanaa saw her mother die.

"There was a man, in the truck, he got out of the truck and came to us. He was wearing black stuff. Mama called out to him for help, I think he wanted to help, he pulled the glass from mama's neck, but she only bled more," said Sanaa.

"There was someone?" Janet jerked up and looked at Sanaa.

"He said to me if I ever tell anyone that I saw him, he would kill me." Sanaa looked at Janet with her watery eyes. "What if he knows I told you? Janet, I'm scared."

"It's okay; he won't know you told me." Janet felt her stomach knot up. Was it a coincidence that Sanaa and her mother were hit by a truck on a Sunday or not? "Did you see his face?" Janet asked. Sanaa nodded.

"He looked scary; he had a scar on his cheek."

"What?" Janet's lip started quivering. She felt like she was going to be sick. Tears rolled down her face as she pulled Sanaa into her arms. She couldn't believe the coincidence. She sobbed quietly and squeezed Sanaa tightly. Sanaa was also crying.

Sanaa stopped crying and just fell asleep. Janet slowly climbed out of bed and headed out of the room. Still in her pajama bottoms and a white T-shirt, she rushed upstairs, walked through the kitchen and into the dining room. The maids looked at her as though she had gone crazy, but she didn't care. Janet walked up the stairs, her legs shaking like jelly and fists squeezed tightly. She knocked on the sheikh's bedroom door.

"What?" he called out. Janet stood at the door, shaking like a leaf, but she needed to talk to him. The door opened, and Janet looked up at the sheikh. He was wearing a pair of silk pajama bottoms without a shirt on.

"Janet?" He raised an eyebrow. "What are you doing here? At this time, not dressed properly?"

"I need to talk to you." Her voice shook.

The Sheikh's Second Chance

"Can't it wait?"

"No." Janet walked into his bedroom. It was her first time in there. It was large, much larger than Sanaa's. His king-sized bed was unmade; he had probably gotten straight out of bed to answer the door.

"Um," Janet cleared her throat. The sheikh narrowed his gaze at her.

"You caused so much fuss already; you might as well say whatever you have to say."

Janet took a deep breath. "You asked me what I did before I started working here," she said.

"You worked at a shipping company." The sheikh crossed his arms over his chest.

"I didn't quite tell you everything."

"Okay?"

"I worked for a cartel," she said. She looked up at the sheikh. "I didn't know at first, but then when I found out, it was too late. I couldn't quit. The only way I could leave was in a body bag."

"I see," the sheikh replied.

"One day, I overheard my boss talking to his right-hand man, talking about Sunday and a family. I didn't know what he was talking about at first, but then when he asked me to buy a truck for him, it clicked. I wanted to say no, but he was adamant. He wanted it as soon as possible."

"Why are you telling me this?" Janet's eyes welled up. The sheikh raised his eyebrows. "Why are you crying?" He looked so concerned; it broke Janet's heart.

"I ran away af...after that. I...I...never went back to work and moved away from Corpus Christi." Janet's voice trembled as she spoke. Tears flowed down her cheeks. The sheikh moved closer to her and held her shoulders.

"You did the right thing," he said to her. Janet shook her head.

"This morning, Sanaa crawled into my bed."

"She did?" The sheikh raised an eyebrow. "She never sleeps with anyone, not even me."

"She told me about the day...her mother...died." Janet was struggling to say the words out loud, but she knew that she had to.

"She did?"

Janet nodded. "A truck hit their car," she said.

"I know that."

Janet took a few steps back from the sheikh. She didn't deserve his kindness. After what she had done, he shouldn't have been the one to comfort her. She wiped her tears and took a deep breath.

"Sanaa stopped talking was because the truck driver told her that he'd kill her if she told anyone that she saw him," said Janet. The sheikh crossed his eyebrows, and the veins in his neck became apparent.

"What?" he said. His voice got deeper.

"She described him to me," Janet paused. "He works for the cartel, and he's the right-hand man of the boss."

"What are you saying right now?"

"The cartel killed your wife, I'm so sorry." Janet burst into tears. "I'm so sorry." Janet covered her face with her hands and sobbed. She felt so horrible. She felt like it was all her fault that Sanaa's mother had died, and because of her Sanaa could have been killed too.

"I'll pack my things and go. I understand if you never want to see me again," she said.

"No," said the sheikh.

"What do you mean?"

"Do they know you're here?"

Janet shook her head. "I don't think so, but I can't risk it. I have already done something unforgivable."

"Stay, if you leave then who will look after Sanaa? She can't lose someone else she loves."

"Sanaa," Janet whispered. More tears rolled down her face. The poor little girl didn't deserve any of that. Janet closed her eyes and ran her hands through her hair. "I love her, too; I can't believe I'm the cause of her pain."

"What's the name of this cartel?" he asked her.

"Jimenez cartel."

"Damn," the sheikh swore under his breath.

"I'm sorry." Janet ran out of his room. She felt so bad; she couldn't even look at him.

Chapter 13

Basil was paralyzed with shock for a moment; he couldn't believe what Janet had just told him. For months, they tried to find the hit-and-run driver who killed his wife, but they couldn't. Now Janet was telling him that she knew who did it? And his daughter saw who did it?

So many emotions coursed through Basil and in a fit of rage, he swiped everything off his dressing table to the floor. He picked up the dressing table stool and threw it at the door. He was so angry; he wanted to punch someone. The Jimenez cartel specifically. Initially, he had thought the accident was indeed an accident; then, he investigated any possible enemies or rivalries he had.

Basil walked over to the other side of his bed and picked up his phone, which was on the nightstand. He swiped the screen and called a number. He put the phone to his ear as he walked towards the sliding glass doors. He slid the door open and walked onto the veranda.

"Hello," the other person answered the phone.

"We need to talk," said Basil.

"Okay, did something happen?"

"Yes, be at my house as soon as you can."

"Alright."

Basil hung up the phone and then went back into his bedroom. He changed into sports shorts and a T-shirt. He headed out of his bedroom and went down to his gym. He had a large gym in his house, on the ground floor. The gym was arranged into three sections. From the door going to the right were lifting weights. On the left side from the door were a treadmill and other exercise machines. In the middle of the room was a large mat where he did his kickboxing and floor exercises.

Basil walked over to a rack with boxing gloves. He picked up a pair and put them on. He walked onto the mat and started punching and kicking the punching bag. Kickboxing or swimming was often the best way for him to let his anger or frustrations out.

It was about half an hour later when a maid knocked on the door. "You have a visitor," she said to the sheikh. Basil stopped boxing and turned around. A tall man dressed in a black shirt and a pair of black trousers walked into the room with his hands in his pockets. His dark hair was tied into a low ponytail. He had a neatly trimmed beard.

"You're kickboxing; this can't be good," said the man. His voice was quite hoarse.

"Tariq," said Basil. He took his gloves off and threw them on the floor. He started walking towards Tariq.

"Can I get you anything?" the maid asked. She was still standing in the doorway.

"Leave us," Basil said to her.

"Yes, sheikh." The small, timid maid shut the door before she left. Just near the door was a water dispenser. Basil filled a cup with water and gulped it down.

"You're sweating a lot, how long have you been at it?" Tariq asked. Tariq had worked for Basil's family for a long time as part of the security team. Even though he had moved on and opened his own private investigation firm, he still came to Basil's aid whenever he needed him. They were also friends. They just didn't often meet because of their busy schedules.

"We need to talk about Rania," he said. Tariq raised his dark eyebrows.

"You want to talk about your wife?"

"About who killed her."

"I have failed you, Basil. I haven't been able to find out who was behind the accident."

"I know who did it."

Tariq raised an eyebrow.

The Sheikh's Second Chance

"And it wasn't an accident either." Basil ran his hand through his hair. He then told Tariq everything Janet had told him.

"That's insane." Tariq was in disbelief.

"I know. I couldn't believe it either," said Basil.

"Can we trust her words? I mean, how well do you know this woman?" Tariq looked suspicious. "I can look into her life, see what I can find."

Basil dismissed him. "She wasn't lying." Basil drank some more water.

"Why are you trusting her words so easily?"

"My daughter was part of the truth coming out. It makes sense, that was the reason why she stopped talking. You know Sanaa. Before the accident, she was full of life, but then she stopped talking or playing with toys. She completely changed." Basil justified his reason for trusting Janet. It had been a few months since she had come into his life and he felt as though he knew her and could trust her. He had seen how hard it was for her to tell him the truth.

"I thought there wasn't a feud between the Jimenez cartel and us. They had been living quietly for a while," said Tariq.

"I guess I'll have to end it," said Basil.

The Sheikh's Second Chance

***

It had been a few days since Basil had found out who was behind his wife's death. He had left home for a few days. He had matters to take care of, and he needed time to gather his thoughts. His next move needed to be executed properly. The feud needed to end. Before he had left his home, he made sure that Janet and Sanaa were safe. There were extra security guards watching the house.

Basil parked outside a motel and got out of the car. He looked at a piece of paper in his hand. "Room 70," he mumbled to himself. He ran up the stairs and searched for the room he needed. He knocked on the door when he found it.

"Who is it?" someone called out from behind the door. The door swung open, revealing a fair-skinned woman. Her hair was neatly pinned into a low bun. She was wearing a calf-length black dress. She looked to be in her mid-forties.

"Hello," Basil greeted her.

"Hello, how can I help you?"

Basil could see a little girl in the room, sitting on the sofa, looking at the door. The woman closed the door a little bit, to stop Basil from seeing the little girl.

"My name is Basil, your daughter works for me," he said gently. He could tell that she was intimidated by him, slightly scared.

"Basil?" She raised an eyebrow. He nodded.

"Her current boss. She looks after my child."

"Oh, what brings you over?"

"I believe we need to talk. May I come in?"

Basil walked into the small room and sat down on the sofa, next to the little girl. "You must be Kim," he said to her with a smile.

"Who are you?" Kim asked him.

"Can I get you anything?" Esther, Janet's mother, asked him.

"No, thank you."

There was only a two-seater sofa in the room, so she had to get a chair from the corner of the room and bring it closer, so that it was opposite Basil. She sat down on the chair. Kim stood up from the sofa and went to stand next to her mother.

"Did Janet do something wrong?" she asked.

"No, quite the opposite. She's been great with my girl. I'm grateful," Basil replied.

"I see." She smiled. "But what brings you over here?"

"Janet told me the reason why you left Corpus Christi."

"What?" Esther gasped. She placed her hand on her heart, and the color drained from her face.

"It's alright, I want to help," said Basil. He tried his best to be gentle, because he could sense that Esther and Kim were scared.

"Thank you, but we'll be fine."

"No, you won't. The cartel is very dangerous; you won't be able to handle them on your own. It's only a matter of time until they find you. I'd rather that didn't happen."

Esther's eyes raced. "How do I know that you're really Janet's boss and not part of the cartel?" she asked. Fair question, he thought to himself.

"Janet said her boss was handthum," said Kim. Basil couldn't help but smile at the way she lisped the word handsome. He was also intrigued by Janet telling her family that she thought he was handsome.

"You don't think I'm handsome?" Basil asked her.

"You are." She covered her mouth and giggled.

"Stop it." Esther nudged her daughter.

"You can look for me online," said Basil. Esther didn't say anything for a moment; she took her phone out of her pocket. She searched for Basil online. She smiled.

"I only searched Sheikh Basil since I didn't know your last name, but you came up in the search anyway." She put the phone down. "I'm sorry, but I have to be sure," she said.

"I understand."

"So, she told you about her previous job?"

"Yes, and that's why I'm here. Those men are very dangerous. I can't let you stay here."

"We've been staying here safely. We'll be okay," said Esther.

"It took me less than two days to find you," he said. With help from Tariq, he had been able to track down Esther and Kim. "I have my car outside; I'm not leaving without you both," he added. Besides his concern for their safety, Basil didn't want to leave them in the motel because it wasn't a nice place to stay.

"Your daughter told me everything about the cartel. She trusted me; can you trust me too?" he asked. Esther and Kim looked at each other.

"I can't just come with you. I don't want to burden you," said Esther.

"It's not a burden," he replied.

Esther was silent for a moment. "We'll only come with you because Janet wanted us to move to Dallas anyway. I feel ashamed of getting help from you like this," she said.

"There's nothing to be ashamed of," he said.

"Where will you take us?" she asked.

"To my home."

Esther raised her eyebrows. "We can stay at a motel nearby," she said.

"No, that defeats the purpose of me trying to keep you safe."

Esther sighed. "We'll have to trouble you then. As soon as we can, we'll leave. Thank you for your kindness," she said.

"It's fine. I owe Janet for being great with my daughter."

Esther smiled. "She has always been good with children. She's very kind and honest," she said.

"I know."

"Kim, go pack your stuff," Esther said to her daughter.

"Okay." Kim went over to the closet and started packing her stuff.

"Will the cartel not find us at your house?" Esther asked Basil.

"They might, but they wouldn't dare do anything to you while you are in my house."

Esther raised her eyebrows. "You're not into any shady business, are you? Why wouldn't they dare?" she asked.

"Harming me will bring a lot of enemies to the cartel." He shrugged his shoulders. He was from a powerful and wealthy family. They had connections in many parts of the world. Besides all that, Basil was prepared to protect Janet at all costs.

Chapter 14

Janet was sitting in the living room with Sanaa watching TV. Sanaa was leaning against Janet, holding her hand. Janet felt guilty over how Sanaa was cuddling her and just being so close to her when she was part of the reason that her mother died. Janet blamed herself, if she hadn't purchased that truck then maybe Sanaa's mother would still be alive.

The sheikh was probably upset with her. She hadn't spoken to him since Sunday morning when she had told him everything about the cartel. He had left on a *trip*. Janet didn't think he had gone on a work-related trip. He probably just wanted to be away from her.

"Janet!" She heard a squeaky voice call out. Janet whipped her head around so fast because she recognized the voice.

"Kimmie?" Janet jumped up to her feet. Her little sister ran into her arms. "How did you get here?"

"Hey, Janet." Janet looked up and saw her mother standing in the doorway.

"Ma?" Like a little girl, Janet ran to her mother and wrapped her arms around her. She had missed her so much. It wasn't easy for her being far away and not being able to see her.

The Sheikh's Second Chance

"My sweet girl," said her mother. She hugged Janet tightly and kissed her on the forehead. Janet stayed in her mother's embrace for a moment. She just breathed in her sweet scent and cuddled up to her mom.

Janet pulled out of her mother's embrace. "How did you get here?" she asked. Just before her mother could answer, the sheikh appeared in the doorway.

"Hi, Daddy!" Sanaa called out.

"Hey, habibti." The sheikh smiled at her.

Janet looked at the sheikh. It was her first time seeing him in four days and not seeing him for that long stirred up all kinds of emotions inside her. She felt guilty for her part in his wife's death. She didn't like not seeing him for that long. She had gotten used to seeing him every day, even if it was for a short time. She liked being able to see him and talk to him.

"Sheikh," she said quietly. She looked at the ground. Janet's mother crossed her eyebrows and looked at Janet and then at the sheikh.

"We need to talk," he said. Janet nodded in response. They needed to talk indeed. The sheikh turned around and started walking. Janet followed the sheikh out and down the hall. He headed to the patio and slid the glass doors open. When Janet joined him outside, he slid the doors shut.

"Um..." Janet didn't know what to say.

The Sheikh's Second Chance

"After what you told me, I thought that your mother and sister wouldn't be safe from the cartel," said the sheikh. Janet looked up.

"How did you find them?" she asked. She had never told him exactly where they were living.

"I have my ways," he said.

"I will find a place for them to stay." Janet wasn't sure why the sheikh had brought her family over and didn't know how to ask him.

"No," Basil shook his head. He leaned against a wooden pillar with his hands in his pockets and his gaze fixed on Janet. "There are plenty of guest rooms in this house; they can stay here. It's safer," he said.

"Oh no, we can't trouble you like this."

"You're not; it was my choice. I'm sorry I made it without talking to you first, but I just worried about their safety."

"Why are you worried about their safety? After what I did…"

"You did nothing wrong," the sheikh cut her off.

"If I hadn't bought that truck," Janet paused to fight back the tears. She didn't want to start crying in front of him again.

"Then Pablo would have bought a truck anyway and probably would have harmed you."

The Sheikh's Second Chance

"I could have tried to stop him or something."

Basil raised an eyebrow. "Janet," he said. Hearing her name on his lips brought happiness and sadness to her heart. She liked it when he called her name, but she didn't deserve it.

"You know how the cartel works. When the boss tells you to jump, you jump. There's nothing you could have done to stop him," said the sheikh.

Janet knew he was right, but she couldn't help but feel guilty. She ran her hand through her curly hair.

"Damnit," she cursed under her breath as the tears flowed down her cheeks. "I'm really sorry. What can I do to make up for it? Tell me, and I'll do it," she said to the sheikh.

The sheikh sighed before he closed the distance between them. He put his hand to her face and wiped her cheek with his thumb. "How did you work for the cartel when you're this sensitive?" he asked.

"I'm sorry." More tears flowed down her cheeks. The sheikh pulled her into his arms and held her tightly. Janet was shocked by the sheikh suddenly hugging her, but she couldn't push him away, she didn't want to. She rested against his chest and cried for a little bit. The sheikh gently stroked her back and held her tighter.

Janet wrapped her arms around the sheikh and just hugged him back. She felt comfortable and safe in his arms. He smelled and felt good. She felt like pulling him back into her arms when he pulled out of her embrace. He cupped her chin and tilted her head up.

"It's not your fault," he said to her. Janet searched his eyes. She didn't understand why he was so nice to her. He caressed her face with his thumb and traced her jawline. Janet wasn't sure what to do or say. She felt butterflies in her stomach. She thought of running away, but he had his hands on her face.

"Sheikh," she said quietly.

"Basil," he said.

"Huh?"

"Call me Basil."

Janet raised her eyebrows. He wanted her to call him by his name. She had wanted to call him by his name for a while, she didn't like calling him sheikh. It was so formal.

Basil leaned closer to Janet until their faces were inches away from each other. Janet was surprised by his sudden movement. She felt even more nervous; her breathing became uneven. Basil placed his hands on her waist and pulled her closer to him. He pressed his lips against hers and slowly kissed her. Janet froze in place for a moment.

She relaxed and allowed herself to kiss him. She placed her hands on his large biceps and kissed him back. For a moment, it wasn't the sheikh and the nanny; it was just Basil and Janet. For a moment, she just wanted to enjoy kissing him and be in his arms.

Janet pulled herself away from him and took a few steps back. "Um," she ran her hand through her hair and looked away. As much as she wanted to be in Basil's strong arms and kissing him, she knew that she didn't deserve him.

Basil took a few steps back and leaned against the wooden pillar. "You went from being this talkative and outgoing person to a shy one," Basil teased. Janet turned her head and faced him. She crossed her arms over her chest.

"You can't blame me for suddenly becoming shy. The kiss was unexpected," she said.

"Was it?"

"Ah…" Janet trailed off. She didn't know what to say. "I have to go check on everyone." She turned on her heel and ran back into the house.

She walked into the living room, visibly flustered. Her mother was sitting on the sofa with her hands laced together. Kim was sitting next to her, and Sanaa was just standing in the distance.

"Is everything okay?" Janet's mother asked her.

"Yes," Janet replied. She wanted to scream that no, it wasn't alright, because it wasn't. She had just kissed

The Sheikh's Second Chance

Basil, and it was amazing. She didn't know if she had feelings for him or what to do now. She was just a mess, and she needed to talk to someone. However, with children in the room, she couldn't.

"Hi, everyone," said Janet. Sanaa walked over to her and stood by her side. She looked at Janet's mother and then up at Janet. "That's my mother and my sister." Janet smiled at Sanaa.

"I tried to talk to her earlier," Kim confessed to Janet.

"The two of you are the same age," Janet said to Kim and Sanaa. The two girls looked at each other awkwardly. Sanaa wasn't as outgoing as Kim was. She didn't easily open up to people. Janet placed her hands on her hips and sighed. Her life was one big mess. Having her family in the same house as the sheikh and Sanaa was going to be a giant awkward situation she wasn't ready for.

Chapter 15

Janet woke up and quickly took a shower and got dressed in a navy-blue T-shirt and a pair of jeans. She slipped on a pair of ballet flats and headed out of her room. As she walked past the living room, she saw Sanaa and Kim sitting in there watching TV. She crossed her eyebrows and went to investigate.

"Morning, girls," she said.

"Hi," they chorused. The two of them were still wearing their pajamas.

"What's going on in here?"

"I asked Sanaa if we could watch TV," said Kim. Janet wasn't surprised that it was Kim that had initiated the entire thing. Her little sister was very outgoing and friendly.

"Where's ma?" Janet asked.

"Outside with my daddy," Sanaa replied. Kim nodded her head in agreement.

"Huh?" Janet wasn't expecting to hear that. It was only 9 a.m., and everyone had already woken up and started their day. "Okay, play nice with each other. I'll be right back." Janet rushed down the corridor. She slid the glass doors open and walked out.

The Sheikh's Second Chance

Her mother and the sheikh were sitting down at the table drinking tea. Janet wondered what they were talking about.

"Morning, sheikh," Janet greeted Basil.

"Morning," he replied.

"Hi, Ma."

"Hi, Janet," her mother replied. The sheikh rose to his feet with his cup in his hand.

"I suppose I should leave you both to catch up," he said. He walked towards Janet, who stood in the doorway.

"Have you had breakfast?" Janet asked him. She wanted to ask him if he slept well, take his hand, hug him, kiss him. However, she couldn't do that. She wasn't sure where she stood with him, and she knew that she didn't deserve him.

"I have." Basil touched Janet's arm. "You should eat too and relax. You look tense."

Janet smiled and nodded. Basil walked into the house and shut the door behind him. Janet went to sit down next to her mother.

"How long have you and the sheikh been dating?" her mother asked.

"What? Nothing is going on between us," Janet replied. Her mother narrowed her gaze at her.

The Sheikh's Second Chance

"I'm not blind."

"Honestly, we're not dating and we are not in any kind of relationship."

Her mother said nothing for a moment. She just looked at Janet and then smiled. "He's a good man," she said.

"What makes you say that? What were the two of you talking about at such an early time?"

"He brought Kim and me here for two reasons, according to him. He wanted us to be safe, and he needed me to be there for you. He thinks you're having a hard time with knowing who killed Sanaa's mother."

"He said that?" Janet was having a hard time, indeed. She was sad and felt guilty, but she didn't know that the sheikh knew or cared.

"He deeply cares for you. I believe he came to find us because of his love for you. I don't think he'd have done that for someone else."

Janet ran her hand through her hair and crossed her arms over her chest. "All I did was work at a shipping company, and then my life turned upside down," she said. Her mother took Janet's hand into hers.

"There's no use crying over spilt milk. What's done is done. Just be good to him and Sanaa. That's how you can repay his kindness," said her mother. Janet nodded.

"I have to go into town," said Janet. "I need to go to town to pick up Sanaa's inhaler." Sanaa's inhaler was almost empty and it was time to pick up another from a pharmacy.

"Alright, do you need me to come with you?"

"No, I'll be back soon." Janet touched her mother on the shoulder before she went into the house. She checked on the girls before she left. Sanaa and Kim were still watching TV together. Janet smiled at the sight of Sanaa and Kim hanging out together. She had a feeling that her sister would bring Sanaa out of her shell.

Janet walked off and headed out of the house. She quickly walked down the driveway and then headed out of the gates. She wanted to get to town and return quickly.

She walked down a long road which led to town. The road wasn't so busy, it was a quiet residential area. Janet thought about Basil, about that kiss they had shared the night before. Janet traced her face with her fingertips and then traced her lips. Basil had caressed her face and stared into her eyes. Janet giggled to herself.

Suddenly, she saw a black Camaro stop in front of her. Janet remembered seeing it a week earlier. The window rolled down, and a man poked his head out. "Excuse me, sorry to bother you, but I was wondering if you could direct me to the bus station," he said to her so politely with a smile on his face.

"Oh, the bus station." Janet tucked a lock of hair behind her ear and stopped walking. She lowered her head so that she could talk to the driver and direct him to the station.

Janet's heart stopped when she saw a familiar man sitting in the passenger's seat. His cold gaze gave her shivers. It was one face she had hoped never to see ever again.

"Long time no see," he said to her. He lifted his shirt, flashing a gun that was tucked into his belt. "Don't even think about running," he said.

"Mateo," she breathed. When Janet had seen that black Camaro the week before, it just hadn't set right with her. The man she had seen had scared her. She had seen him staring at her and then he followed her back to the sheikh's house.

"Pablo has been looking for you," said Mateo. Janet's stomach knotted up. She didn't know what to do. She wanted to run away, but she knew that she wouldn't get far. Mateo was in a car and had a gun.

"Why? I wasn't worth anything." Her voice trembled. She tried so hard to speak in a normal tone, but she was struggling.

"Get in."

"No."

"Janet, you wouldn't dare argue with me," he warned.

The driver got out of the car and grabbed Janet's arm. "Get off me," she cried out desperately. He pulled her and opened the backseat car door and shoved her into the car. He shut the door and got into the front seat. Janet sat up and saw Mateo pointing a gun at her.

"Sit still," he said. The driver got into the car and drove off. Janet's eyes welled up. Her worst nightmare was coming to reality. When she ran away from Corpus Christi, she knew that the choice she had made would get her killed if she was caught. She knew too much about the cartel's business to be left to live freely.

The driver sped up the car and Janet couldn't even figure out where they were going. Or maybe because she was frightened, she couldn't think of what to do. She didn't know how to save herself.

They arrived at some warehouse by the river. Mateo got out of the car and opened the backseat door for Janet. He pulled her out of the car and shoved her. "Move," he said. Janet tried to run, but he grabbed her arm before she could get away. He slapped her across the face. "Behave!" he said. Janet touched her face where he'd hit her. He picked her up and threw her over his shoulder. He carried her into the big warehouse.

Mateo threw Janet onto the floor. Janet looked around the warehouse. There was nothing in there except four members of the cartel. They were all glaring at her and grinning.

"You have some balls on, little lady," she heard a voice say. She instantly knew who it was. Pablo. Janet turned and saw him walking into the warehouse.

"Pablo," she said as tears flowed down her face.

"You dared to do what most men wouldn't do, leave the cartel," he said.

"I was only your secretary. I wasn't really part of the cartel. I didn't mean anything to you or your business." She tried to plead with Pablo by making him realize that she was too insignificant to kill.

Pablo approached her and stood above her looking down at her. "You know far too much for me to keep you alive," he said to her.

"I won't tell anyone anything, please let me go."

Pablo crouched down and leveled his face with hers. She could smell the cigarettes and cheap cologne. The smell just made her sick. "All this time, you've been living with Basil. That's another reason for me to kill you," he said.

The Sheikh's Second Chance

"Basil? I just work as a housemaid, that is all."

"For Basil though." His expression grew dark and scary. Janet wondered how Pablo knew Basil. He seemed to hate the fact that she worked for Basil. It didn't make sense to her why he was bothered by that.

"Mateo, shall we kill her slowly or quickly?" Pablo asked his right-hand man.

"Slowly, she doesn't deserve the mercy of a quick death," Mateo replied. His scar deepened as he smiled at Janet. His smile gave her shivers. The other men were leaning against the wall, watching the entire thing.

"I agree," said Pablo. "I liked you, you know." Pablo pulled out a long steel knife out of his pocket. He took out his handkerchief and wiped it slowly while keeping eye contact with Janet.

In that moment, all Janet could think about was Basil. She didn't want to die before she had the chance to be with him. She had known him for a short while, but he had quickly become an important part of her life. She had gotten used to seeing him every day and spending time with him on the patio.

More tears rolled down her cheeks as she mourned the relationship that hadn't gotten a chance to begin. Janet also felt sad about leaving Sanaa alone. She had grown to love the little girl. She couldn't bear not being able to see her again.

At least my family is safe, she thought to herself. She was glad that they were under the care of the sheikh. She didn't want anything to happen to them.

"Before I kill you, I need to know why you ran away," Pablo said to her. Janet swallowed before she answered.

"I knew what you were going to use that truck for, and I didn't want to be a part of that or work for someone who kills people."

Pablo gave her half a smile. In a swift movement, he cut Janet's arm, causing her to scream out in pain. "It's sharp enough," Pablo said, looking at the knife and smiling in satisfaction.

Suddenly, the metal door of the warehouse was flung open. Janet screamed and hugged herself and looked down. She thought more members of the cartel were coming in.

"Back away from her right now." Janet heard a familiar voice.

Chapter 16

Janet looked at Basil standing in the doorway. Pablo rose to his feet and squared his shoulders. "Basil," he said.

"Touch another hair on her head, and I'll kill you myself," said Basil.

"Basil!" Janet cried out. "It's not safe here; you should go."

"Yeah, Basil, you should go," Mateo said mockingly, imitating Janet's voice. The other members of the cartel laughed in response.

"Let's see if you'll be laughing in a minute." The sheikh walked into the warehouse with authority, head held up high and shoulders squared. Janet was scared for him; it wasn't safe there with the cartel. She didn't want anything to happen to Basil; she would never forgive herself.

"FBI!" A group of officers dressed in bulletproof vests ran into the warehouse with guns in their hands.

"What?" Pablo spat out. The color drained from his face as he saw the FBI officers running into the warehouse. He tried to reach for his gun, but then Basil approached him and punched him in the face. Janet gasped as Pablo staggered backwards. He came back in full force and swung for Basil, but Basil blocked his fist.

Basil punched him a few times before he kicked him. Pablo fell to the floor with blood trickling down from his nose. Mateo tried to get involved but was stopped by an unfamiliar man with a ponytail and a beard. The other members of the cartel were getting cuffed by the FBI.

"We'll take it from here, sheikh," one of the FBI officers said to the sheikh.

Basil got down to one knee in front of Janet. "Are you okay?" he asked. Janet searched his eyes before she threw her arms around his neck. She was so happy to see him. When Pablo was about to kill her, Basil's face was the last to flash in her mind. The thought of never being able to see him again was terrifying for her.

"I'm okay," Janet said. She held on to Basil tightly as the tears fell down her face. Basil pulled her out of his embrace and did a quick inspection. He saw blood on her right arm.

"That bastard," Basil swore. Janet smiled and shook her head.

"I'm okay, don't worry about that little wound," she said to him. She reached out and touched his face.

"You're safe now; I'll never let you get hurt again," he said.

The Sheikh's Second Chance

Janet heard the officers arresting Pablo for kidnapping and attempted murder, for ordering a hit on Basil's wife and for smuggling drugs. They handcuffed him.

"I hope you rot in jail. You should have stayed away from my family when I warned you. Now you got what you deserved, you piece of crap," Basil said to Pablo.

"You will regret this!" Pablo spat out in outrage.

"No, you will regret not staying in your lane and coming after me. I'm ending this nonsense feud, don't even try to harm my family or my business. If so, not only you but your entire family will pay the price." Basil's voice was deeper and scarier. Pablo turned red in the face, he looked so angry.

Basil returned his attention to Janet. In one swift movement, he scooped her up into his arms. Janet squeaked at the sudden lift. She wrapped her arms around his neck and allowed him to carry her out of the warehouse. His car was parked outside. He put her into the passenger's seat and buckled her in. Janet watched him being so caring with her; it was adorable.

"I'm glad you're okay." Basil cupped her chin and pulled her face towards his. He pressed his lips against her. Janet smiled and ran her hand through his hair.

Basil closed the door and then walked around the car and got into the driver's seat. He started the car engine and drove off.

"How did you find me?" Janet asked Basil.

"After you told me about the cartel, I had extra security around the house and had someone keep an eye on you whenever you left the house," he said. Janet raised her eyebrows.

"You weren't scared of the cartel?" Janet asked Basil.

"No."

"You said that you were ending the nonsense feud. What did you mean by that?"

Basil sighed before he responded. "Well, his grandfather and mine were once business partners," he said.

"Really?" Janet gasped. Basil nodded as he took a right turn.

"Fady, my grandfather wanted to extend our business into Mexico, thirty years ago. That's when he met Carlos, Pablo's grandfather."

Fady wanted to break into the Mexican market as an oil supplier. Carlos was an ambitious man who wanted to expand his transport and shipping company. Fady saw potential in him and decided to partner with him, giving him a chance to extend his reach into El-Tabas.

The Sheikh's Second Chance

Fady was able to transport oil into Mexico using Carlos' services. However, their partnership ended when Carlos started smuggling drugs into El-Tabas. When Fady found out what Carlos was doing, he terminated the partnership and used his family connections to make sure that Carlos couldn't do business in El-Tabas or other Middle Eastern countries ever again. He even got all his ships confiscated by the El-Tabas government. A few years later, Carlos tried to have Fady killed when he visited Mexico. The feud trickled down to their children and grandchildren.

"Wow, that is crazy," said Janet. She was shocked that Basil's family and the cartel had had a feud for so long.

"So, even if you didn't buy that truck, he was always going to find a way to try and kill me," said Basil.

"What will happen to him now?"

"Well, the FBI has been trying to arrest him for years. He should go to jail for killing Rania, kidnapping and attempting to kill you, drug trafficking and other murders he's responsible for. We don't have to worry about him ever again."

Janet sighed with relief. She was glad that it was all over. Working for Pablo had been a nightmare for her. Finally, she was free from him, and it was all thanks to Basil.

The Sheikh's Second Chance

They arrived at the sheikh's house and parked outside the front door. They both got out of the car.

"Does my mom know what's been happening?" Janet asked Basil before she opened the front door.

"No, I didn't get the chance to tell her. I just wanted to get to you as soon as I could," he replied. Janet stood on her toes and kissed Basil on his cheek. She was touched that he cared for her and had just saved her life.

Basil held the back of her head and kissed her. Janet placed her hands on his chest and kissed him back. Basil opened the front door and picked up Janet into his arms. She kicked the door shut and he headed up the stairs with Janet in his arms.

"Where are you taking me?" she asked him. She started giggling.

"Shhh, if you laugh loudly, then Sanaa will hear you, and if she hears you, she'll run to you."

"What's wrong with that?"

"You spend time with her all the time; it's my turn now."

Janet laughed even more. "That's so immature, Basil," she said. He smiled and shrugged his shoulders in response. They walked down the corridor and reached Basil's bedroom. He opened the door and walked in. He kicked the door shut and set Janet down on his bed.

He walked off into the bathroom and returned with a small first-aid kit. He placed it on the bed and rolled up Janet's T-shirt.

"It's not bad," she said to him. He took out a cotton ball and dabbed it in an antiseptic solution and cleaned her cut gently. Janet watched him cleaning it and then putting a bandage over it. Janet kissed him on the forehead.

"Thank you," she said. Basil put the kit on the nightstand when he finished. He got onto the bed next to her and caressed her face.

"I'll never let anyone hurt you again," he said. Janet searched his eyes.

"You're good to me," she said. Basil kissed her hands.

"You're so beautiful," he said.

"Am I?"

"Of course." Basil leaned in and kissed her cheek.

"What's beautiful about me?"

"Your face," he kissed her jaw. "You have beautiful eyes, lips, cheekbones."

"What else?" Janet giggled.

"Your skin is beautiful." He ran his hand down her side. "Your body, your heart. Everything about you is perfect." He caressed her thighs.

"So, you just love me, that's what you're saying?"

Basil smiled and kissed the back of her hand. "I do love you so much. I don't know what I'd have done if I had lost you today," he said. Janet stroked his face and searched his eyes.

"I love you too," she said. She'd never said those words to anyone who wasn't family. She'd never had feelings for anyone like that. She was truly happy and in love with Basil.

***

A few days later, Basil parked his car just in front of the beautiful white house. He grabbed the flowers and got out of the car. He walked into the house and heard voices coming from the living room. He headed over to the living room and saw Sanaa and Kim in there, talking about their meeting schedule for the fall.

"I finish school at 3; I can come right after," said Sanaa.

"That works for me but what do we do about weekends?" Kim replied. The two of them looked so serious as if they were discussing something so important. Basil smiled to himself. Sanaa and Kim had known each other for such a short time, but they had quickly bonded. Basil was happy seeing his daughter have a close friend.

"Hi." Janet walked into the living room and approached Basil.

"Hi," he replied with a smile. He looked at Janet from head to toe. She was wearing a yellow summer dress and had her hair down. It was his first time seeing her in a dress, and he thought she looked so beautiful.

"You're gorgeous," he said.

"Am I?" Janet smiled and tucked a lock of hair behind her ear.

"Hmm." Basil stared at Janet. He wanted to hold her and kiss her.

"Why are you two staring at each other like that?" said Esther as she walked into the room.

"Hi, Esther," Basil greeted her. He kissed her on both cheeks and handed her flowers.

"You bought me flowers?" Esther smiled.

"Yes, I bought flowers for my beautiful ladies." He handed Janet her flowers and then approached Sanaa and Kim. "Flowers for the princesses," he said as he handed them both flowers.

"Thank you," Sanaa and Kim said in chorus. Basil smiled and patted both of them on the head.

"Do you like the house?" he asked Esther.

"Yes, it's amazing. Thank you so much," she replied. Basil had bought a house for Janet's family since Janet wanted them to move to Dallas. Janet had protested and begged him not to buy a house for them, but Basil was adamant. For him, it was something small. He wanted to do that and more for Janet. If she asked him to go to the moon for her, he would, in a heartbeat. He was so blessed to have a second chance for love and having a complete family.

"You don't have to thank me. If you need anything, just let me know," Basil replied.

"Let's go and do your room," Sanaa said to Kim. The two of them held hands and walked out of the room with their flowers in their hands.

"They're so adorable," Janet smiled as she watched Sanaa and Kim walking away together.

"They are," Basil agreed.

"So how long have you been dating?" Esther asked Basil and Janet.

"Huh?" Janet was caught off guard by her mother's question.

"I still have yet to take her out on a proper date," Basil replied.

"You haven't?" Esther was surprised.

"No, I'm not very good at courting. You'll have to help me."

"Of course."

Basil looked at Janet and took her hand into his. "I want you to be my woman, not Sanaa's nanny. I want you to be at my side forever," he said.

"I want you to be my man too," she said shyly.

"Aww," Esther placed her hands on her heart. "Thank you for helping us with the cartel. We owe you so much for being there for us." She smiled and rubbed Basil's arm. Basil smiled back at her. She walked out of the room.

"We do owe you," said Janet. Basil pulled her closer to him and placed his hands on her waist.

"You can pay me back by giving me a kiss." Basil dipped his head and kissed Janet.

"I love you," she whispered against his mouth.

"I love you."

What to read next?

If you liked this book, you will also like *In Love with a Haunted House*. Another interesting book is *The Oil Prince*.

In Love With a Haunted House

The last thing Mallory Clark wants to do is move back home. She has no choice, though, since the company she worked for in Chicago has just downsized her, and everybody else. To make matters worse her fiancé has broken their engagement, and her heart, leaving her hurting and scarred. When her mother tells her that the house she always coveted as a child, the once-famed Gray Oaks Manor, is not only on the market but selling for a song, it seems to Mallory that the best thing she could possibly do would be to put Chicago, and everything and everyone in it, behind her. Arriving back home she runs into gorgeous and mysterious Blake Hunter. Blake is new to town and like her he is interested in buying the crumbling old Victorian on the edge of the historic downtown center, although his reasons are his own. Blake is instantly intrigued by the flame-haired beauty with the fiery temper and the vulnerable expression in her eyes. He can feel the attraction between them and knows it is mutual, but he also knows that the last thing on earth he needs is to get involved with a woman determined to take away a house he has to have.

The Oil Prince

A car drives over a puddle and muddy water splashes Emily, who was just out for a walk, from head to toe. When she sees the car parked at a gas station moments later, she decides to confront the man leaning against it. The handsome man refuses to apologize, and after hearing what Emily thinks about him, watches her leave. The next day, fate plays a joke on Emily when she finds out that the man is her boss's brother and a prince of a Middle Eastern country. Prince Basil often appears in tabloids because of different scandals and in order to tame his temper, his father sends him to work on a project of drilling a methane well in Dallas. If Basil refuses or is unsuccessful, his financial accounts will be blocked and his title of prince will be revoked. Although their characters clash, Emily and Basil fall in love while working together and Basil's heart melts. When the project that can significantly improve his family business hits a major obstacle, Basil proves that love has tremendous power and shows a side of himself that nobody knew existed.

About Kate Goldman

In childhood I observed a huge love between my mother and father and promised myself that one day I would meet a man whom I would fall in love with head over heels. At the age of 16, I wrote my first romance story that was published in a student magazine and was read by my entire neighborhood. I enjoy writing romance stories that readers can turn into captivating imaginary movies where characters fall in love, overcome difficult obstacles, and participate in best adventures of their lives. Most of the time you can find me reading a great fiction book in a cozy armchair, writing a romance story in a hammock near the ocean, or traveling around the world with my beloved husband.

One Last Thing…

If you believe that *The Sheikh's Second Chance i*s worth sharing, would you spend a minute to let your friends know about it?

If this book lets them have a great time, they will be enormously grateful to you – as will I.

Kate

www.KateGoldmanBooks.com

Printed in Dunstable, United Kingdom